THE TURQUOISE SERPENT

Ashes of the Urn 1

ALEXANDER PALACIO

Copyright © 2020 by Alexander Palacio

All rights reserved.

No part of this book may be reproduced in any form or by any electronic or mechanical means, including information storage and retrieval systems, without written permission from the author, except for the use of brief quotations in a book review.

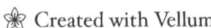 Created with Vellum

For the boys

THE TURQUOISE SERPENT

heads bulged and towered, blotting out the weak winter sun and sweeping toward the caravan, driven by the cackling wind.

Cayucali shouted for the captain of the troop and received the butt of a spear in his back for his trouble. It was a gentle prod. The guard was trying to be respectful. It didn't help.

"That storm will blow us off the mountain," Cayucali said.

"Captain Siyaj knows his business," the soldier laughed. "Never been rained on, flatlander? Besides, only one road to follow."

"We could follow it faster," Cayucali grumbled.

The King's men were mad, as far as he was concerned. He thought of them as mountain goats, ornery and unpredictable. The coasts of his youth in Tolcalax, the low hills of his exile—these were lands suitable for men. The cold heights of high mountains were where goats grazed on tough grasses and broad-pinioned condors built hidden eyries. But if the heights bothered any of the King's soldiers, they didn't show it, so neither would he. And if they all looked too young to know the name of the kingdom to whose old borders they even now drew dangerously near, he had no reason to remind them.

He bore them no particular malice, but he felt no urge to aid his own hangmen. Chimal had made his capital at Batun, in the heart of the mountains, and it was there Cayucali would be tried, sentenced, and executed. He resolved to demand a lesser sentence to account for the torture of crossing the high pass. And worse, through land of such black fame.

The captain seemed finally to take heed of the storm when Cayucali felt the first fine droplets of rain against his cheek. He cried out a command and Cayucali felt the butt of the spear prod his back again.

"Double march," his guard said.

The High Pass

Stones shifted, soil sank. The edge of the path crumbled away beneath Cayucali's sandaled foot, a cascade of earth down the steep cliffside. The sound of the scree was lost in the howl of rising wind that dragged the warrior toward the edge. He hunched his broad frame in the greedy wind and pressed himself against the stern face of the mountain.

His wrists were tied. Before him and behind him on the narrow path, his guards made their own efforts to shelter against the wind. Every man in the caravan was lashed together by strong rope, lest one should fall. Even still, Cayucali had no interest in dangling from his waist, hands bound, like a fat tomato still on the vine. Besides, he was by far the biggest man in the caravan and nursed a secret worry that if he fell, he would pull the others into the void with him. The face of the mountain offered the illusion of safety.

The wind rose, moaning like a dying man. The path merged into the darkening sky, vanishing into the gloom as it followed the curve of the mountain. Cayucali lifted his gaze from the wizard to the turbulent heavens. Anvil thunder-

Perhaps he did bear some malice afterall. Certainly toward the magician's whelp who walked at the head of the column, near the captain. The boy looked like a tadpole, hopping along with his broken arms bound across his chest. Cayucali grinned to himself, but his heart wasn't in it. There was no thrill of battle in the memory of cracking the young wizard's arms. He wondered whether violating his exile had been worth it. He shook his head. It had all been worth it to see Saqui again, even for a moment. At least she was safe in Tolcalax.

The outer edges of the storm swallowed them quickly. Perhaps the captain did know his route, but Cayucali grew up on a fishing scow. He knew storms, and he knew enough to fear being caught in Xacan's fury. When the goddess' storms passed above his city of Tolcalax to crash against the wall of the mountains, the Tolcalaxtin had the good sense to go inside.

These mountain goats had no good sense. As the wind whipped higher and the rain began to fall in earnest, the sky darkened and bolts of lightning tore ragged streaks through the iron sky. Cayucali could not help but laugh as a finger of lightning illuminated the boy wizard wriggling forward, unable to shield his eyes from the driving rain.

As treacherous as the path had been under clear skies, it grew a hundredfold more dangerous as the storm engulfed them. The narrow path grew soft and slippery. Mud sucked at their feet and seemed to pull them toward the edge of the cliff. The rain blinded them and the wind blew against their packs and tested their balance. Little runnels of water streamed from the stone face of the mountain and seemed to erode the earthen path beneath their feet. Where the path was stone, it was slick and polished and treacherous.

The deluge grew fiercer. Even his captors seemed cowed by Xacan's fury. Raindrops swarmed around them, buzzing and stinging like bees. The wind lashed and curled and snapped like a whip. Thunder shook the earth and lightning scorched the air until it seemed burned and ruined to breathe.

The guard in front of Cayucali slipped in the wet mud. Cayucali hardly heard the scream, but he felt the tug on his waist, felt himself lurch headlong toward the edge of the cliff. He fell to his knees and planted his hands in the sucking mud. In a flash of lightning, he saw the next man in line do the same. The column halted. Orders came, relayed man to man, down the line.

"Pull him up!"

Cayucali could hardly hear the command above the scream of the wind. It did not matter; he already had the rope in his hands. The gale curled around the next soldier's pack and he stumbled toward the lip of the precipice. Cayucali lunged. He caught the man by his belt with one hand. The other remained curled around the coarse rope. The skin of his palm burned. The soldier nodded to him, then took up the rope again.

"Pull!" he shouted.

They fished the fallen man out of the abyss and set him on his feet. His face was ashen, his gaze blank. He trembled and hove great breaths as he stared dumbly into the driving rain. His fellows grinned, slapped his shoulder, and the column continued its march. Cayucali shook his head once more at the madness of mountain goats.

The storm rose further, scourging the impassive face of the mountain with deranged fury. Then their pace slowed, though they were still far from the high pass that led to Batun. Cayucali thought they must come to a stop and huddle into the mountain until the storm spent itself. The caravan could withstand no more. Yet suddenly, the men ahead of him seemed to disappear into the very stone. He halted, then stumbled forward as the rope at his waist dragged him into a black crevasse hidden in a fold of the rock.

Cayucali found himself in a narrow cavern, damp, cold, but rainless and windless. He wiped the water from his eyes and released a tense breath. Safe, for now.

The Tunnel

※

"Did I not tell you, Warlord? The captain knows his business."

The soldier was gloating behind him, wringing out his tunic and humming to himself. Cayucali did not care. The captain did seem to know his business, and Cayucali was grateful. In gratitude, and to avoid the butt of the spear, he kept his mouth shut and followed the caravan deeper into the mountain. The passage was pitch black, but the floor was smooth and level. He stretched his wrists, bound together still, and let his fingers trace the walls that pressed close on either side. His touch told him the tunnel was hewn by the hand of man, not born of the mountain itself. The scars of chisel and hammer were shallow gouges and long lines in the soft stone.

Then the wall drifted out of his reach. He felt a room open around him, tasted the different scents in the air and heard the tiny distinction in the echo of his footfall. But the column did not stop.

"We have food. Will we camp while the storm passes? How long do they last in the mountains?" Cayucali waited for the butt of the spear, but it never came. Instead, the guard chuckled.

"Too long for camping and waiting. These caves pass beneath the mountain. A shortcut to Batun."

Cayucali almost stumbled.

"Beneath the mountain? You said the captain knew his business. We need to take the high pass. We should camp and wait for the storm to die."

"A prisoner does not set our course."

"Let me talk to the Captain Siyaj. He leads us into cursed lands. Unsafe lands. It is better to wait out the storm."

Now came the jab from the butt of the spear. Cayucali's jaw clenched. He tested the bonds that tied his wrists and fingered the knots in the rope at his waist. The captain might want to lead them to their deaths, and the boy wizard was welcome to it, but Cayucali had an audience with King Chimal, and he suddenly wanted to keep it. But the ropes were thick, and the knots were tight.

They trudged through the tunnel for several hours before the stale air became fresh once more. They emerged through a narrow portal that seemed, after a few steps, to disappear into the rock behind them. On this side of the mountain a few wispy clouds, underlit with the embers of sunset, obscured the emerging stars. Only a faint breeze recalled the wild rage of Xacan's storm still raging to the east, beating ineffectually against the mountain's vast wall.

Here, the slope was milder. The troop untied the ropes that bound each man together. Except for the ropes that bound Cayucali to his two guards—he was a prisoner, after all, bound for trial in Batun for violating an edict of exile. The captain called a double march from the head of the column. Cayucali watched Tezca, the boy wizard, climb wearily to his feet. He grimaced when he had to put his shoulder against a tree. More than a boy, maybe, but less than a man. Still slim, still gawky. Probably he always would be—wizards spent all their time squinting at old books and talking to themselves.

As the column began to trot down the faint path into the cool, dense jungle of the valley below, Cayucali thought he should have used the edge of the blade instead of the flat. He stared hard at the dark forest, letting old instincts awaken, straining his eyes for the flash of blackglass, the sway of leaves against the wind.

The captain should know better than to stray into this cursed and ruined land. He risked the displeasure of those who might still remain in it. Yet the captain led them down from the mountains and into the forest, following the sun that even now slipped beneath the high collar of the mountains to the west. Somewhere beyond those peaks was Batun, the seat of Chimal's power, from which he would issue judgment for what Cayucali had done. There could only be one verdict, and one sentence. It would come quickly, and be carried out with kind swiftness and admirable regret. Better than what happened to those who tarried too long or spoke too loudly in the haunted forests they now transversed.

Then the column came upon a place of ruins, a clearing in the damp, cold forest. The stars shone on high stone walls and rotted wooden beams. The roof of the thing had half fallen away, but enough remained to promise shelter. Cayucali knew it was coming, but he still groaned when the captain called a halt. The column made camp quickly, efficiently, digging dry wood from beneath the leaf cover and arranging their packs to protect the nascent flame from the wind that meandered among the fallen stones and through the gaps in the walls like worms through the sockets of a skull.

His captors lashed him to a broken column, its stone circumference sheared away a head above his own height. He was too distant from the campfire to enjoy the comfort of its warmth but more than close enough to share in the danger it posed. Around the fire, Chimal's soldiers ate road rations and passed a clay bottle from man to man.

"Captain!" he called. "I know this place. We must continue through the night. We are in danger here."

Captain Siyaj wiped his lips, stood, and picked his way across the rubble-strewn mosaic floor to the broken pillar. He offered the bottle to Cayucali. From the flared lip came the intense scent of ferment and sweet honey. Cayucali shook his head. The captain shrugged and took another drink. He was older than the rest of the column, but still younger than Cayucali. He looked capable, but Cayucali could see the cheery film of drunkenness creeping across his face.

"With this shortcut, we have time to rest. Jungle is dangerous at the night. My men, they are tired. Jaguars. Poisonous snakes. Hungry things."

"We are in the Serpent Kingdom, Captain. We are in Kalak Mool. Do they still tell the tales in Batun?"

"Grandmothers do," the captain laughed. "Men know better than to believe in vampires and devils. Batun destroyed the armies of Kalak. You see the proof of that around you now. That war is over."

The captain returned to the fire and passed the clay bottle to the next man. Cayucali shook his head as he slid down the pillar and sat upon the stone pedestal. "This was a kingdom of sorcerers, Captain," Cayucali said, as loud as he dared. "Perhaps it still is. You cannot trust everything you see."

The Ruined Temple

※

Tezca put his back against the crumbling stone wall and pushed himself to his feet. The pressure against his shoulders sent little spears of fire through his broken arms, but the honey liquor Captain Siyaj passed around dulled the pain somewhat.

"Magician!" one of the soldiers called. "Make the colors dance!"

Tezca grimaced. It was hard to draw even that simple sigil with the toe of his sandal in the dirt. But keeping his escort happy seemed wise. Whatever the captain said, he had a strange feeling about this shortcut. He traced the glyph in the dust near the fire and connected it to the campfire with a tendril of his own warmth. The sigil exploded into a kaleidoscope of rainbow colors and scintillating flames. The soldiers chatted and drank. The prisoner glowered at him from his broken pillar. Suddenly encouraged, he smiled at the bound savage and pushed the iridescent flames to even greater displays of color.

When the savage turned away, he again lost interest in the game. He put the dancing fire behind him and wandered through the ruined buildings, picking his way carefully through the uneven terrain. In the days since the column left Tolcalax, he had learned to be careful about his footing. Falling, a minor annoyance a week ago, was now his biggest fear. He had slipped once, on the way up the mountain. By instinct, he tried to stretch out his arms to catch himself. Straining against the bandages that bound his broken arms to his chest was agony. Then he hit the ground. The memory of that pain, and the sight of that stupid savage laughing at him, kept him warm even without the fire.

It didn't matter. He would be home soon. His arms would heal. The savage would be executed. Master Tall-Deer might not like how he handled the provincials in Tolcalax, but Master Tall-Deer served at his father's pleasure. No more stations in vassal-cities. No more provincial governors. He would learn the highest sigils and he would become the Master of the King's secret libraries.

He let these gloating thoughts carry him across the yard and into another structure. This ruin was less decayed than that which sheltered the caravan, but much smaller. Or it seemed smaller, until he began to explore within. It had no back wall; rather, passages continued into passages, linking ever-larger rooms together like a tangled pearl necklace.

There was some undetectable incline at work that led him ever farther into the skin of the earth. He was now deep beneath the surface in caverns cut from living stone and lit by dense clusters of worms that fed on lichen growing on the moist rock. These, Tezca inspected for some time, fascinated by their beautiful colors and lonely existence.

From deeper down the passage, he heard some rhythmic sound. He let himself be drawn downward by curiosity. The sound resolved into a rhythmic pounding, a gigantic heartbeat in stone. Then, the greenish light of the glowworms was mixed with orange. The faintest of firelights played on the walls, now roughly hewn instead of finely worked as they had been above. He followed the weaving orange and yellow into the next passage.

He emerged into a colossal cavern. He stood on a high gallery, a narrow ledge that seemed to stretch around the circumference of the great room. From his perch, he could see the source of the sound and light that had drawn him thither. It came from below; the cavern was full of men attired for war. They were arrayed around a monstrous altar, on either side of which fires burned in braziers of carved stone. Behind the altar, naked figures hammered against massive drums.

Then another figure, robed and hooded, appeared before the altar. He seemed to coalesce from the hazy darkness, slipping along the tongues of firelight until he stood between the two braziers. He commanded the attention of the rapt attendees. Tezca knelt carefully against the wall of the passage to watch.

The man flung away his vestment and stood nude in the punishing heat of the two braziers. His bronze skin shone with sweat as he lifted his hands above his head. The heartbeat drumming ceased. Those gathered around the altar fell to their knees and pressed their heads against the floor of the cavern in obeisance.

Then the strange priest turned and began to circle the altar. He cast handfuls of some profane alchemies into the braziers, and they belched forth a choking liquescent smoke. The acrid fumes unsteadied Tezca's head even high above the ritual, and when the drumming began again, it pounded through his body as if it were his own heartbeat.

The men in the cavern below bore long knives of some gleaming bluish stone. Bracing himself for the inevitable pain, he put his back to the narrow wall of the passage and began to push himself to his feet. It was past time to go. He had often dreamed of discovering some hidden knowledge. But now that he had it, Tezca was not at all certain it was wise to keep it to himself. He had to warn Captain Siyaj and the King's escort.

But then the drumming paused again. The cavern was full of maddening incense, and the priest's bare chest heaved in frenzy. He lifted his hands. His powerful voice thundered through the stone chamber. Tezca found himself unable to move, pinned to the wall like an insect by the power of the priest's invocation. Though the dialect was archaic and unfamiliar, it seemed to make itself known to him as he listened.

The Ritual

❧

"You who kneel here, remain! The rite begins. Xicuoatl, the Turquoise Serpent, thirsts! And we must nourish him, and so nourish ourselves, and Kalak Mool. The time of celestial agreement is close—with our sacrifice, the serpent will shed its skin once more!"

The priest's speech filled the room. Echoes lingered, then faded as the drumming began again. The priest stalked again to the altar and hurled more of the incense into the braziers. He wiped sweat from his brow with his arm and began making certain preparations of the altar. He swept it clean with a small brush, then pressed his forehead to the stone and knelt there for long minutes, chanting a sinister incantation that seemed to writhe and curl around Tezca like the coils of an anaconda.

He tried again to move, but some great fist was clenched about him. A fat spider crawled across his fingers, the tiny hooks of its feet prickling his skin, yet he could not lift his hands to flick the arachnid away. His breath seemed to still, his lungs to deflate. Some infernal resonance rose in his chest; the drums pounded, and he pounded with them.

Movement in the cavern below drew his attention again.

A knot of men fought their way toward the altar, dragging a struggling shape between them. The wicked blue stone knives swung at their belts, but the men were gentle with their captive, bearing the blows as they climbed the steps to where the priest had risen from the altar. Most of the men withdrew, leaving two holding the captive by the arms. The priest ripped the linen robe from the captive, who now stood naked before the assembled worshippers. It was a woman.

She struggled against her captors once again, seeming nearly to break away from them, though where she thought to flee after winning her freedom, Tezca could not guess. Nor did he discover the answer. The men kept their hold on the woman and dragged her to the altar. There, each kept hold of an arm or a leg. They bore their weight upon her limbs so that she was still and stretched across the face of the altar.

Her scream broke whatever spell kept Tezca immobilized. Bile rose in his chest and his heart suddenly accelerated far beyond the pace of the drumming. He climbed to his feet, choking back a groan as his shoulders dragged against the stone passageway. He turned to retrace his steps, but inexplicably found himself drawn deeper into the cavern. He crept out onto the narrow ledge, following the curve of the cavern wall as it led nearer the altar.

As he sidled along, he moved deeper into some strange field, some energetic presence. It seemed to call to him, to welcome him, to bend beneath his weight the way water bent beneath the little oarsmen bugs that stroked across the surface of Tall-Deer's garden pond. He was intoxicated.

Then a scream ripped from the altar. That thrilling, wrenching, echoing sound marked the plunge of the priest's knife into the woman's bare breast. Disgusted yet awed, Tezca watched the priest make a precise incision. The woman jerked, then stilled. Her captors stood and bowed away from the altar. The priest pushed his hands into the incision and cracked the ribcage open. His forearms were bright with blood. He lifted the heart high above his head, then, incanting blessings over it, divided it in two and fed it to the burning braziers.

Wicked curls of a suffocating black smoke roiled from the braziers. The presence Tezca felt before grew stronger, but seemed to release its grip on him. He began to inch away from the altar, along the high ledge, back toward the passage. He could hardly see it through the black smoke. He was not a pious man, but he whispered an imprecation to Tlaoc for protection just in case.

The smoke now poured from the braziers in great undulating waves, pulsing outward like the ocean tide, coursing and licking up the walls of the cavern hungrily. He crept toward the opening as quickly as he could, but the smoke outpaced him. Where it touched him, the same resonance he had felt before seemed to bellow through his bones. His body rang like a hammer-struck bell. He was sure he would fall from the ledge into the assembled soldiers below. It was all he could do to cling to the rough stone wall, only steps away from the safety of the passage.

The priest felt the resonance. Tezca knew he must burn like a beacon to that hateful conjuror. And no sooner did the mystical chimes ring out from him than had the priest spotted him, illuminated by the flames that devoured the sacrificial heart. Their eyes met. The blinding smoke cleared, drawn from the cavern by some unseen chimney. Tezca saw a stern face alight with the passion of the ritual. Black eyes swam with command. An elegant hand, blooddrenched and shining, pointed at him. The sharp voice cracked like a whip.

"The serpent has brought us a gift! Alight, little bird! Flutter down, and all will be well."

Tezca only pushed himself harder against the wall, ignoring the pain in his shoulders. As the smoke dispersed, so did the possessing presence. He took one step toward the passage, then another. Then he was inside, following the pinched hallway as quickly as his trembling legs would allow. He had to get back to the camp. He blinked endlessly, his eyes burning with smoke, burning with the image of the screaming, struggling woman, burning with the jewel-red gleam of the bloody heart.

The priest's shout carried through the passage. "Bring him to me!"

Then there was the sound of thunder, and Tezca knew it was the thunder of a hundred blood-mad worshippers chasing him through the shadowy ruins. He sprinted through the dark building, heedless of the danger of falling. Broken arms were better than whatever fate awaited him if he failed to reach the King's escort in time.

The thunder rolled again, closer this time.

Puncture

❦

Cayucali's mood was foul. His skull ached with the pulse of sorcery. The fetid stench of it filled his nostrils. It had begun with the boy wizard's juvenile conjuring; the puerile colors waggling and sparkling, the increasingly intoxicated soldiers cheering at the insipid display. The colors in the fire faded, but the stench remained. In fact, it grew worse. What was the whelp doing? Ensorcelling some demon to confound and vex him, he did not doubt.

But there was nothing he could do about it. Whatever the boy was doing, he was doing it out of sight. And Cayucali was still tied around the broken pillar. He slumped against the pedestal, trying to find a comfortable position. He drew deep breaths, but the tension did not leave the knotted muscles of his back. The dull tapping pain at the back of his head did not cease. He glowered at the world.

The captain rose from the circle of soldiers. The fire silhouetted him against the bright stars as he moved toward the pillar. He swayed a little under the effects of the honey liquor, but stood steadily enough as he stared down at Cayucali. He paused for a moment, then circled the pillar. Cayucali struggled to his feet. His shoulders tingled. His arms were asleep.

Stone bit against stone and something fell to the earth. His arms swung free. The captain moved back around the pillar.

"Come sit by the fire, Warlord," the captain said. "Have a drink with us."

Cayucali stretched his arms, worked blood back into his limbs. He stayed seated against the pedestal of the pillar.

"No," Cayucali said. "The magician and I do not get along."

"You behaved yourself for fifteen years. Why not another night? Besides, Master Tezca has retired, or keeps his own company. He left the fire over an hour ago."

Cayucali stood. He towered above the captain, stretched his thick arms high above his head. He arched his spine like a jaguar, then shook himself all over. He accepted the bottle of honey liquor from the captain and took a drink.

"It is cold tonight," he said, and together they sat at the campfire. One man tossed him a strip of dried tapir. He ripped at it with his teeth and grunted in satisfaction and thanks. Cayucali passed some minutes in silence. He drank in the warmth of the fire, savoring the sweet bite of the honey liquor and the rich taste of the fat summer tapir. The stars wheeled slowly overhead. The wind wandered through the tops of the trees, flicking at leaves like a bored boy swinging a branch.

"We are sorry to keep your wrists bound, Warlord," the captain said. "The King commanded that you be accorded the greatest respect."

"King Chimal shows me great courtesy. As do you. Yet it is always wise to keep your prisoners bound."

"I hardly remember the Morning War. I was only a boy." The captain waved a hand in a gesture encompassing the two dozen or so soldiers camping in the ruin. "The men are too young to remember."

"It was a long time ago," Cayucali said.

"What was it like?"

Cayucali leaned back and turned his face to the sky. Dark fingers of cloud stretched across the stars. The throb in his skull was back, worse than ever. What was that puling spellbinder playing with? Whatever it was, Kalak Mool was the wrong place to do it. The serpent kingdom had earned a serpent's reputation during the Morning War.

"Like a dream," he said. "Like a nightmare. We could not tell night from day, reality from illusion. We could not tell life from death."

A few of the men moved toward the fire and seated themselves nearby, but Cayucali had no stomach for war stories. Especially not here, within the lands of the serpent. The soldiers sensed his reserve. His silence seemed a sufficient answer to their questions. The fire spat and cracked.

The silence stretched, then broke. Cayucali surged to his feet, every muscle trembling, before he knew what was wrong. Captain Siyaj followed closely behind him. He slashed the air for silence. A chorus of shouts rose from the darkness beyond the fire.

"Who is it?" he hissed. "These lands are dead."

"Death has a bargain with Kalak Mool," Cayucali said.

"Tamoc, douse the fire," the captain said.

"Weapons," Cayucali growled. "Where is my sword? Give it to me. Cut my bonds."

The captain ignored him. "We must not be caught here. Make for the border. Leave the camp. Move fast." He surveyed the dwindling campfire and the courtyard strewn with half-empty packs. "Where is the wizard?"

"Drawing down some curse on me," Cayucali said, turning to follow. "Leave him."

The captain nodded. "No choice."

Then there were sudden footfalls in the courtyard, and panicked, gasping breaths. Stone-edged blades whispered from their sheaths. Tezca collapsed at the edge of the firelight. Captain Siyaj caught him. The chorus of shouts grew louder.

"Soldiers," Tezca gasped. "A hundred. Maybe more."

"Who? Where?"

"Underground. They are mad. A bloody ritual..." Tezca shuddered.

The cacophonous shouting crested. The man called Tamoc jerked and groaned. He pitched forward, scattering the coals of the fire. A short wooden spear thrust from his spine like the quill of a porcupine. His clothes smoked and the air was full of the sour smell of burning wool.

Then a sea of shades writhed on the edges of the courtyard. The worshippers from the ruin flooded into the courtyard and the camp exploded into chaos. The captain shoved Tezca toward a hole in the ruined wall and called a retreat. The King's escort collapsed into a bristling knot. The worshippers crashed against them and were hurled back.

In the confusion of that first collision, Cayucali lost sight of the captain. Another spear buzzed past him, driven by the hard swing of a throwing club. Then the man was upon him, swinging the club at his legs. He stepped away from its arc and kicked the man's legs out from beneath him. He rolled beneath another falling club, then leapt a crumbled fragment of the courtyard wall and sped away into deeper shadows.

Blue Knives

❦

Bloodlust gripped the ruins. The shadows boiled with knots of men locked in struggle. Bodies were strewn among the ancient stones and creeping vines. Pale moonflowers folded their petals, or else were stained by spurting black blood. The coals of the campfire cast eerie fingers of warm light onto the muted tableau.

Cayucali sought the deepest shadows. He moved carefully, taking his time, keeping his back to the crumbling stone walls when he could. The sounds of thickest fighting moved away from him, drifting northward. Captain Siyaj lead the caravan toward the distant border. They would never make it across.

Few of the attackers noticed him. They streamed from out of the darkness, following the sounds of fighting, heedless of the dark shape moving slowly in the wrong direction. Presently, Cayucali came to a structure more intact than most of the others. The attackers streamed from this ruin, bursting from its black mouth like bats. Despite their feverish excitement, they were soldiers trained. He could see it in their motions, their bearing, the way they coursed as a pack toward the retreating caravan.

Then something different came out from the ruin and

into the night. Torches. A circle of stern men ringed an older man. He was gowned in soft cotton, dyed white and worked in the colors of Kalak Mool. He walked with a slight limp, leaning on a tall soldier who walked at his side. Cayucali watched the priest say something to the tall soldier, who swung his head. The priest patted his arm in a fatherly gesture. Beneath the gown's embroidered sleeves, the priest's hands were bloodstained. Beneath the silvery hood, his mouth was bloodstained. The tall soldier nodded once, then loped away into the night, chasing the caravan. The old priest limped after, and his escort followed.

Cayucali slipped around the corner of the ruin, making for the deep shadows at the fringe of the forest. A strong hand fell on his shoulder. He felt himself spun around. He glimpsed one of the attackers and brought his hands up just in time to stop blade chipped of some strange blue glass thrusting toward his belly.

He caught the man's wrist in his hands and squeezed until he felt the bones grind together. The man's face contorted into a mask of pain in the moonlight. Then, remembering himself, he opened his mouth to cry the alarm. Cayucali pulled the man toward himself and hammered the crown of his skull into the shocked face. Hot blood fountained and the sentry slumped to the earth.

The blue glass blade stuck in the soil at his feet. Cayucali plucked up the blade and pressed himself against the wall of the ruin. No outcry came from the courtyard. He drew the knife against the ropes that bound his wrists. They fell away, and Cayucali sprang up the side of the ruin like a monkey. He moved with startling quickness, pantherine and lithe, until he flattened himself out along a corner of the roof to stare down at the courtyard below.

The ruins spread out beneath him like writing on a scroll. Stone washed in cool moonlight leapt out in contrast against the low, dark foliage that choked the clearing. Around the clearing, the forest stretched for long leagues until it crashed like waves against the bulwark of the high mountains. The sky above the mountains was clear. They should have waited in the tunnel.

Cayucali marked the limping priest. He passed with his escort near the place where the coals of the fire still smoldered. Orange tints leapt across his white gown in lurid splashes of color. A few soldiers remained beside him; the rest of the host streamed like hunting wolves forward through the ruins and into a gap in the trees where an overgrown road marked the shortest way to the border of Batun. The priest stopped for a moment at the coals of the fire. He murmured, gestured, and pastel colors leapt from the fire in ghostly imitation of the jewel tones the boy conjured before the attack. Seemingly satisfied, the priest stood and stalked away into the night.

Cayucali's spine hummed at the bloom of magic. He reached for a sword that was not there. His keen ears sought and found the sound of fighting. Somewhere in the dark night, the caravan still fought its doomed retreat. A great shame. The captain was a decent soldier. If he were smart, he would cut the wizard loose. A few of them might make it out.

The courtyard was empty now. He pushed himself up and crouched on the corner of the roof. To anyone watching from beneath, he would be a hulking black gargoyle against the stars. He looked back toward the mountains—toward the small crack in the great stone wall that led back to the road and back to Tolcalax.

He dropped silently to the earth. The sentry was still there, sleeping unwillingly. Cayucali kicked him over so he would not drown in his bloody nose and took the leather sheath for the blue glass knife from his chest. He wished he had his sword. He replayed the strange image of the priest near the fire, conjuring an echo of Tezca's colored flames.

Something about that disturbed him. The priest seemed like he was looking for confirmation of something, and found it. What did Kalak Mool want with that miserable little spell-wright Tezca?

He drifted through the courtyard like a ghost. He claimed a fallen pack and stuffed it with abandoned road rations. He found the tapir strips scattered in the dirt around the dying coals. He brushed them off and ate several of them. He claimed another knife from the chest of one of King Chimal's fallen soldiers. It slid from his ribcage with a sucking sound. Chimal's men acquitted themselves fiercely. The courtyard was littered with fallen blue knives. Cayucali left them to live or die, as they would.

He crossed to the edge of the forest. Faint shouts filtered through the trees from the road to Batun. He wished the captain luck, then vanished into the dark jungle.

Standoff

Tezca fell hard. The earth was soft beneath him, but no cushion could soften the pain of falling on broken arms. He screamed. Wet mud filled his mouth.

Captain Siyaj jerked him back to his feet. His face was a stone mask.

"Can you do nothing? No spell, no sorcery to aid us?"

Tezca swung his head. Spellcraft took time, artistry, focus. The captain could not understand. There was contempt naked on his face.

"Then at least do not slow us," he said.

Tezca nodded. He nearly stumbled again, but caught himself. The stumble saved his life. A spear whirred through the air just above his head and buried itself in the bole of a cacao tree.

"How much farther to the border?" Tezca gasped.

"Too far," the captain said.

Tezca blinked mud from his eyes. A few of the soldiers remained standing. The soldiers of Kalak Mool harried them as they trudged along the overgrown road toward Batun. Now and then, the hunters lunged at openings. The captain left dead men behind them in the mud, losing his own blade in the chest of one of those he slew. The soldiers circled, their bloodlust cooled. They waited.

A tall warrior of Kalak Mool emerged from the darkness. He strode toward them with clear purpose. He glanced at the dying blue knife, then back toward the few remaining soldiers of Batun. His eyes found Tezca, then flicked to the captain. He came forward.

Captain Siyaj cursed. He shrugged the exile Cayucali's ironwood sword from his shoulder. The tip dragged in the mud. He struggled to put the point between himself and the tall warrior.

"Keep moving, Tezca."

Tezca didn't hesitate. If the captain wanted to put himself between Tezca and the enemy, let him. At least he would slow them a little.

Then he felt a new presence. Something huge and dark was suddenly beside him. A thick arm stretched out. A stern voice spoke in a voice of perfect command.

"Give me my sword," the exile said. The captain obeyed.

The tall warrior of Kalak Mood lunged forward. The ironwood blade whipped through the air faster than Tezca's vision could follow. The tall warrior grunted, then sailed through the air and sprawled amid the churned-up muck of the road. Cayucali shouldered the heavy blade and shoved the captain.

"Keep moving or die."

"Warlord," the captain gasped "You returned."

"For all the good it does me," Cayucali said. "Make sure Chimal hears about it. If we make it out, I expect a good word from the boy too. These Blue Knives want him, not us. They won't spare us."

The tall warrior climbed to his feet. He issued quiet orders and the other Blue Knives tightened the knot. When they drew too close, the ironwood blade struck like lightning and taught them fear. It crushed and cut, and the blue glass blades shattered against it. The captain and remaining soldiers of Batun ran with new strength, fought with new fury.

But eventually, it was the land itself that betrayed them. The old road was thick with clutching vines and tendrils. Beneath the foliage, the mud was deep. It sucked at their footsteps and clung to their feet until they were mired hopelessly. Only Cayucali moved without apparent effort.

The Blue Knives flitted through the forest on either side of them. It was pointless to continue fighting against the sucking mud. The Blue Knives sensed their prey was at bay. They ringed the few survivors three deep. The tall warrior pushed through the circle, then turned and shouted an order behind him. He then stood in silence and glared at Cayucali. Whatever fate held in store for them, Tezca suspected Cayucali had done them no favors by embarassing the warrior.

Then the circle parted. A thin figure limped into the road —the priest from the ghastly ritual. Tezca slumped to the ground, pressing himself down into the mud, shrinking away into the low foliage. The priest spread his arms. The black stains of the sacrificial blood painted his hands and his mouth, but he smiled. His voice was calm and warm.

"Enough blood for one night. You have cost me many fine warriors, and lost many of your own. Worse, you nearly interrupted something of . . . great consequence. I offer another way."

Cayucali rested the point of the ironwood blade in the mud and leaned on the pommel.

"Well?" the priest snapped, "Who commands? Who may treat with me? Will you accept my offer?"

"Make your offer," Cayucali grated. "Make it good, or it will cost you more of your fine warriors."

The tall warrior took a step forward, but the priest caught him by the arm.

"The boy is of interest to me. Give him to me. In

exchange, you will not die." He shrugged. "At least, I will not kill you."

Tezca caught the captain's eye. He called to mind everything he had seen in the ruins; the victim's beating heart in the priest's hand, the sinister presence that filled the cavern. He let those images fill his expression as he shook his head at the captain.

"And who are you?" Cayucali asked.

"You know all you need to know about me, warrior," the priest smiled. "And now you must tell me what I need to know. Will you make the wise choice? Will you accept my offer?"

"If you know enough to call me by that title, you know I don't always make the wise choice."

The priest shrugged again. "So be it." He flung out his hands. A fine dust filled the air. He wove his arms in a gentle, flowing pattern and the scintillating dust filled Tezca's eyes, shimmering down toward from above.

Captain Siyaj swayed on his feet, stumbling, then vanished into the thick jungle brush to the side of the road. Cayucali lifted the ironwood blade and started toward the Priest. The tall Blue Knife moved to meet him, but then Cayucali too succumbed. Finally, the cloud of dust settled. Tezca felt himself swimming through the sea of stars above.

"Oahqui," the priest said, his voice broadening into the bellow of the wind itself. He waved the tall Blue Knife forward. "Bring the boy. And the warrior. Kill any others who still live."

Looming warriors filled the sky above him, then the world dissolved into void.

The House of Healing

When his eyes opened again, Tezca stared at a stone ceiling grown thick with flowering vines. It took him several minutes to realize the vines were not living, but carved ornaments. The soft scent of rose was overwhelming. He sat up. His arms were still bound, but for the first time in some weeks, there was no pain in them. He lay on a high stone bier. Cayucali lay on another beside him. The huge warrior began to stir.

There were footsteps in the hall. Tezca lay back down quickly and tried to steady his breath. The footsteps entered the room. Cayucali groaned and shifted on his bier. The footsteps paused, then moved toward him. A gentle voice spoke. A woman's voice.

"You are awake," she said. "Good. The burundanga's soporific effect is powerful. Many never wake. But Itzamma knows his business, as I know mine."

Tezca gave up his charade and opened his eyes. A young woman stood beside Cayucali, staring down at him. Her face was round and lovely, with fine, even features. Long, dark hair covered a slim bronze neck. She wore a modest tunic, unbelted, in a finely woven linen that shimmered in the sunlight that streamed in from the wide doorway. She was beautiful, but Tezca had other concerns.

"Where are we?" he asked.

The woman looked up at him. "Kalak Mool," she said. "The citadel. The house of healing. I am Xhoc. You have been here three days. Your arms are healing quickly. You no longer need those slings."

She unwound the filthy cloth slings that bound his arms to his chest.

"What will you do with us?" Tezca asked as she worked. "Are we your prisoners?"

"I believe you are to meet the King," she said. She pressed her hand against his forehead, her fingers against his wrist. "A rare honor."

"I decline," Cayucali said. He sat up sharply, then grimaced.

Xhoc shook her head. She put her hand on his shoulder and pushed him back down as easily as she might a child.

"The burundanga will make you weak for some time. Rest. All will be well. You will not be harmed in my charge. You are the honored guests of the King of Kalak Mool."

"Kalak Mool was destroyed in the Morning War," Tezca said. He surprised himself with his own recollection of Master Tall-Deer's instruction.

"How can a land be destroyed?" Xhoc smiled. "The land remains and so we remain. We are diminished, it is true. And perhaps those in Batun-at wish us gone. It is not for me to say. But I hope it is not so, and I bear you no malice. It is as I said. You are our honored guests."

Tezca swung his legs over the side of the bier. The cool stone floor felt good against his bare feet.

"Stand, if you can, but slowly. The movement of your blood will help the healing. Only do not try to leave. You must conserve your strength. Itzamma will be here soon."

"Itzamma is here now."

A deep voice came from the doorway. The priest from the ruins limped through the doorway and into the room. Tezca's eyes were drawn inexorably to Itzamma's hands. The bloody horror he had witnessed was still fresh in his mind, but the priest had scoured his hands clean. Now he spread them wide in greeting and bowed deeply.

"Welcome back to the living world," Itzamma said. "Welcome to Kalak Mool. Xhoc tells me you are healing well. That is for the best. I feared you would be injured in your zeal to reject our hospitality."

"Time yet," Cayucali rumbled. His black eyes bored into the priest.

Itzamma suppressed a smile, but it flowered in his sharp eyes. His face was stern and lined, his beard dark with the day's growth. He pressed his hands against his dyed tunic, smoothing it against his chest. Rings of bright silver gleamed on his fingers. A golden clasp held a fine cotton cape across his shoulders. Tezca shivered. The sunlight through the doorway was fading.

"Our hospitality anticipates unwilling guests," Itzamma smiled. "Yet I do hope to win you over. We are truly grateful for your presence. It has the feeling of divine guidance. You are the answer to my prayers."

Itzamma stared at them for a moment longer, then rubbed his hands together and strode briskly toward the far side of the room. There, he busied himself at a long table piled high with the accoutrements of medicine—and surgery. Xhoc hurried to his side. They conferred briefly. She began plucking bundles of fresh herbs from a reed-woven basket. Itzamma added them to a shallow stone bowl and muddled them into a paste.

"What do they want with us?" Tezca whispered. "What do we do?"

Cayucali's brow knitted. He scowled at the ceiling before growling an answer.

"Whatever they want, they must not get it."

"Should we not receive the promised honors? They seem to need us."

Cayucali only sneered.

"Xhoc mended my arms," Tezca said. "It was you who broke them."

"It is right that they were broken. You might have learned something. Now, by dishonest spellcraft, you are captured and deceived by your enemy. It is a flaw of your kind. One of many."

Xhoc returned. In her hands was a bowl. Some fragrant brew filled it.

"Drink some," she said. "It will counter the burundanga. We must go for a walk. Not far, but you are very weak."

"Where?" Cayucali asked.

"Would it mean anything to you if I told you where?" Itzamma snapped.

"It might," Cayucali said. "I have been here before. I have fond memories of my visit."

Some meaning passed between them. Itzamma's mouth tightened for a moment, then he smiled more broadly than ever.

"And it is the Serpent's will that you shall make new ones on your second visit. But come—let me help you to your feet. Lean on me, warrior. You breathed more burundanga than you should have."

Cayucali climbed to his feet unsteadily. Tezca felt Xhoc's hands beneath his shoulders. He sat up and drank from the bowl she held. The taste was mint and rose. Vigor bled through him. He gulped at the bowl. Xhoc laughed and pulled it away from him.

"Slowly, slowly! It is medicine, not beer!"

He smiled, then remembered where he was. Cayucali sniffed the concoction, then took a few cautious sips.

"Wonderful!" Itzamma clapped his hands in delight. "And

now, we will take a short walk, and I promise you answers. Oahqui—"

The tall commander of the blue knives appeared in the doorway.

"—we are expected at the Temple of the Serpent. Lead the way."

Kalak Mool

❦

Oahqui passed through the doorway. Cayucali and Tezca followed him into the golden light of sunset. Tezca stopped, awestruck. They stood in a stone colonnade. On the other side of a long row of columns, the earth dropped away and the Serpent Kingdom unrolled before them. Honey sunlight drenched low hills descending toward a slow river. To the north, a high lake gleamed like a mirror. White-capped mountains marched around the narrow valley, soaring above them in every direction.

In the valley, patchwork fields divided the rich black loam. Low walls of heaped stone or piled branches divided them. Old men and children tended animals who wandered through fields left fallow, or planted thick with field peas. Yet the valley was strangely empty. There were people in the fields, but no homes. No barns. No storehouses or workshops, no temples.

Then Tezca approached the edge of the colonnade. Beneath him the citadel of Kalak Mool fell in stepwise profusion down the side of the mountain. He stood atop a soaring city of hewn and piled stone. Cacophonous structures tumbled away in his vision. Stairways crossed and re-crossed walkways like a nest of petrified snakes. Rooms and houses erupted from the skin of the mountain like toadstools. Tiny patches of tilled soil and planted gardens speckled the citadel like moss on a rock. Kalak Mool was a small mountain itself, perched on the shoulder of a protective mother who loomed to a watchful peak high above.

Cayucali was staring at him, looking thoughtful. It was not a pleasant look. Tezca took a careful step away from the edge.

"Where are we going?"

Oahqui grunted. He stalked away down the colonnade. Itzamma motioned for them to follow. Xhoc walked with them. A cool wind lifted her dark hair. Tezca shivered again.

"To the Temple of the Serpent," Itzamma said. "The heart of the citadel. We are not far. But the stairs may be difficult until the burundanga passes. The medicine should help."

"Why?" Cayucali rumbled. "What business do we have at some profane temple?" He sounded bored, but Tezca was glad he asked.

"Why?" Itzamma was incredulous. "Can you not see why? Are you truly so humbled by age, Warlord? Yes, I recognize you. I will keep your secret from Oahqui. I'm not sure I could keep him from killing you if he knew. But your presence honors Kalak Mool. And the Turquoise Serpent returns honor for honor."

"I have no use for honor anymore."

"Yet honor may still have requirements of you," Itzamma said. He began to limp up a flight of stairs, leaning against Oahqui.

"Where is my sword?"

"It will be returned to you when the time is right."

"And what about me?" Tezca said. "Do you imagine I want some paltry reception from some forgotten township? Do you imagine I will not be missed in Batun? There was a reason I merited a full escort of the King's personal guard."

Itzamma glanced at Cayucali. "You allowed yourself to be captured on his behalf? Do I have the right man?"

Cayucali said nothing.

"Priest," Tezca said. "I am grateful for whatever you did for my broken arms. I will not forget who hurt me or who healed me. Yet I am expected in Batun. You must not delay me." Tezca found himself breathing hard as he climbed another stairway. Ahead of him, Itzamma leaned heavily against Oahqui. The steps were tall and narrow. They passed out from beneath the protective shelter of the colonnade. The wind blew harder in the open.

Itzamma paused for a moment and grimaced in pain. "Your arrival in Batun is indefinitely delayed. Yet wait a little while, and you may one day return home with stature undreamt of."

He began climbing again. The pyramid of the Temple was near. "You do not know where you are. You know nothing of Kalak Mool at all. I can see that in the questions you do not ask."

"Many things are beneath my notice," Tezca said.

"And in Kalak Mool you may reach your greatest heights. Is our little valley not impressive? Our high citadel? It is mostly empty now. It is understandable you know so little of us. We are not what we were. Your friend here had some part in that."

Tezca thought there was a slight grin on Cayucali's motionless face.

"But all of Kalak Mool reveres him for that," Itzamma said. "The Turquoise Serpent has delivered him to us for a reason."

"You have him," Tezca said. "So let me go."

"Let you go? But you are a greater prize even than he," Itzamma said. "Did Xicuoatl, the Turquoise Serpent, not reveal you to me in the cavern, even at the moment he drew closest to the veil? You felt him near, as I did. He called out to you, and you could not help but respond. In you is the potential for divinity. In you is the right to rule. I honor that potential, that right. Kalak Mool honors you. Our King too wishes to honor you. We have awaited your arrival for many years."

"I felt nothing," Tezca stammered. "No one called to me."

Itzamma laughed. The wind tugged at the hem of his bright robe so that he looked like some rare bird. Tezca had felt something. Something terribly cunning, unimaginably old. And something within him rose to greet it.

"Here," Itzamma said. "The last stair." Two Blue Knives stood at a broad stair at the base of the ziggurat. They held long spears and wore black feathers around their arms. Each offered Oahqui a precise salute. Behind Tezca, the vertiginous expanse seemed all too close. Far below, in the house of healing, framed by the colonnade, the heights had seemed picturesque. Now they seemed deadly, immanent.

"You must go first," Itzamma said. He raised his voice to be heard above the constant wind. "It is customary. When you reach the top of the stair, bow, then allow yourself to be seated."

"Seated for what?"

"For the feast," Itzamma said. "Princess, will you join us?"

"My presence was requested," Xhoc said. Then she smiled. Tezca's mouth was suddenly dry. "And I must ensure my patients are not overtaxed. Food will do them good," she said.

"Good," Itzamma said. "Now, up. The King of Kalak Mool awaits your presence."

The Waterlily Throne

⚜

"You must wonder why you are here," the gaunt figure said. He was Yax Yapaat, King of Kalak Mood, Lord of the Serpent Kingdom. He sat across a long wooden table on a divan built from some striped wood and carved all over with waterlilies, the symbol of Kalak Mool's rulers. Cayucali saw the same motif repeated on the linen walls that broke the constant wind, on the banners that flapped on the corners of the summit of the Temple, and on the tunics of the attendants who served at the feast.

Yax Yapaat was pallid, sepulchral. No expression crossed his face, no momentary glimmer of satisfaction at the surfeit of food that suddenly surrounded them. Even his greeting to Xhoc was perfunctory and hollow.

Strange—had Itzamma not called her Princess? Perhaps the word meant something different in Kalak Mool. He tore at a roasted peccary ham and chewed contentedly. First, his sword. Then, a way out.

Beside him, Tezca stood.

"Your highness," he said, "I am Tezcacoyotl. My family is the Grey Ocelot. My father is a counselor to King Chimal of Batun. I thank you for the hospitality you show us. If you would be so kind, your men may escort me to the border and I will make my way to—"

Yax Yapaat stared at Tezca without expression. Itzamma hissed a command to Oahqui, who jerked Tezca back down into his seat without ceremony.

"As my high priest has no doubt explained, you are to be our guests of honor," Yax Yapaat continued. His voice was a hollow rasp. "We shall discuss the particulars of your presence here after our meal. For now, eat. My daughter informs me that food will aid your recovery. The burundanga poison is taxing, but you will soon recuperate."

Attendants circled with trays piled with food. The seats at the long table filled with silent men and women in fine dress. Long capes wrapped around their shoulders. Patterned fur of jaguarundi and agouti kept out the evening chill. Bright feathers rustled when the breeze slipped beneath the linen walls. Hard eyes watched them carefully.

Cayucali ignored them. He stacked bare bones on the table. The Serpent King or his pet priest would speak their piece soon enough. They had plans for him, and he was sure he would not like them. He doubted whether he would eat so well again anytime soon. He knew what kinds of plans the Serpent Kings made. He knew what kind of honors they bestowed. He had plans of his own, and they did not include remaining long in Kalak Mool.

Yet the priest's attitude toward the boy Tezca troubled him. Tezca was a sorcerer, and sorcerors were dangerous fools. Perhaps sorcery could be used wisely, by some great sage well-practiced in virtue and careful in his use of magic. But Cayucali thought not. And Tezca was no great sage anyway.

Yet, he suddenly wished he had not swung his sword and broken the boy's arms. Tezca paid the old king entirely too much attention. He listened with too much interest to whatever Itzamma now whispered in his ear. He cast hateful glances down the table when he thought Cayucali was not looking. And now Cayucali needed Tezca to leave Kalak Mool with him and make a favorable report to Chimal in Batun. He could not return without the whelp.

The Serpent Kingdom was a land of the blackest sorcery. Whatever Yax Yapaat wanted with Tezca, it would ultimately lead to ruin. He knew that as surely as he knew his own name.

He put down another clean bone and leaned to whisper to Tezca. "Play along. When they blink, we will be gone."

Tezca toyed with a knife. He scratched at the floor beneath him, sketching some tangled pattern into the stone with a nervous energy. "We? So you can leave me behind to die? Finish what you started in private?" He dragged the knife in a wide arc, encircling his sketch.

"You earned what I gave you," Cayucali said. "You will get worse here, I promise you. You saw the Serpent Kingdom's way of honoring guests first hand."

"And I see a different way here," Tezca hissed. "Where a King offers me the courtesy due my station."

Just then, Yax Yapaat stood. He lifted a cup set with smooth jade to the darkening sky, then tilted his head back to drink. Those seated around the table followed suit.

"To our esteemed guests from Batun," Yax Yapaat said, "who of course wish to know whether we shall pluck their hearts from their chests. We shall. Or rather, we shall, if they prove worthy of it."

Cayucali rested his forearms on his knees and stared at Tezca, who refused to return his look.

"The warrior will participate in the Liturgy of Coalescence. Itzamma, you will deliver him to Zolin, the Paddockmaster, following the feast." Yax Yapaat regarded Cayucali. "Do you know this liturgy?"

Cayucali shook his head.

"You will fight. The blood you spill will feed the

Turquoise Serpent. Win, and receive the honor to serve as the Champion of the Serpent at the Feast of the Coalescence. Lose, and die."

Cayucali smiled. "I will need my sword."

Yax Yapaat's blank face was unchanging. "You will have it," he rasped. He turned to regard Tezca. The eyes of the other celebrants grew narrow and bright.

"And you, scion of Grey Ocelot," Yax Yapaat said. "You will attend Itzamma, who will see to your remedial education. He informs me you have some aptitude, but little training and less discipline. This must change. Itzamma will see to it."

Itzamma bowed his head.

"My education? I do not understand," Tezca said.

"You yearn for what he can teach you," Yax Yapaat said. "It cannot be otherwise. This is how Kalak Mool shall take your heart. You are a Vessel. I will pray you succeed."

"Succeed? Your highness, I—"

Yax Yapaat waved Tezca into silence. The King looked hollow and faded. His voice neared a whisper. Tezca leaned forward, straining to hear him over the wind. Cayucali slipped a stone knife from the table under his tunic. There was a long pause, then the King spoke again.

"The Serpent has chosen you to succeed me as King of Kalak Mool," he said. "I will pray you succeed that difficult process, for my time is almost over."

There was a quiet sob. Xhoc stood and rushed away from the table, away into the dusk.

A deep silence followed.

The Liturgical Arena

Two Blue Knives shoved Cayucali through a gate of thornwood. A third, the tall Commander Oahqui, slammed the gate shut behind him. Oahqui's stare was venomous.

"The King may call it what he likes," Oahqui said quietly. "But at the Coalescence, I will dance in your skin, and I will take your hands."

"I heard the same thing last time I was here," Cayucali said. He rolled his shoulders and peered down the long passage. A shape took form in the darkness and a man appeared carrying a small, shuttered candle. He was nearly as big as Cayucali, though beginning to stoop with age. He raised one arm in greeting. His cape shifted, revealing that his other arm ended at the elbow.

"Zolin," Oahqui said. "A gift for you from the King. Another celebrant for the Liturgy of Coalescence. See that he is adequately prepared."

The one-armed man saluted. He was a shadow in the hall, but he placed himself between Cayucali and Oahqui's bitter glare. "Thank you, Commander Oahqui," Zolin said. "It will be done."

Oahqui sought out Cayucali over Zolin's shoulder. "I will see you soon, dead man." Then he was gone.

Zolin took Cayucali's arm and led him away from the gate, down the dark passage. His touch was firm, but not hard. There was strength in his remaining arm.

"You're in the Paddock, we call it," Zolin said. "Where celebrants await their turn in the arena. Come with me."

"What does Oahqui command?" Cayucali asked.

"The serpent guard," Zolin said. "The king's finest warriors. Dangerous man. Ambitious, with nowhere higher to go."

The passage widened. Zolin led him into a long hall. Other passages led deeper into the complex; rushlights smoked and quavered in the corners. The empty corridors echoed their footfalls into distorted shuffles.

"Better light during the day," Zolin promised. "Shafts bring sunlight in. We are under the mountain here. Very secure. No chance for escape."

Zolin led him first to the dormitory, a long dark room where lines of wooden bunks stretched away on both sides.

"Find a bed and fall in it—plenty of open spots," Zolin said. Soft snoring filled the darkness, and one or two voices called out sleepy questions. Zolin ignored them, and closed the door again.

He led Cayucali to another room, holding his candle out in front of him. The tiny flame illuminated a grotesque snarl caught in stone. Carved beasts lined the walls and ceiling; every inch of the room was decorated with ornate stonework. The floor was lain thick with reed mats. Mock weaponry filled barrels in the corner of the room, and training stones were ordered neatly along the wall. At the far end of the room, a lean, strong-looking man completed a series of exercises and climbed to his feet.

"Celebrants may train here," Zolin said. "Some do, if they come to us long before their appointed liturgy. The Serpent wishes his celebrants to fight at their best. The King provides them with every necessity. But the liturgy is not what it was. In the old days, hundreds or thousands were kept here. Celebrants lived and trained for years before their appointed liturgy. Now, the celebrants are few."

"Do you miss those days?" Cayucali hefted one of the training stones to his shoulder, then replaced it carefully.

"I am no Kalak," Zolin said. He spoke by rote. "I come from Kapan."

"A fellow vassal of Batun," Cayucali said.

Zolin nodded. "I grew tobacco, once. Now I help supervise the Paddock in exchange for a little more life." He called to the man on the far side of the room. "Pactli! Come meet our newest celebrant."

Pactli crossed to where Zolin and Cayucali stood. He made a gesture of greeting. "You look promising. I trust you will spill a great deal of blood for the honor of the Serpent."

Cayucali snorted. "I don't want to spill any blood for the Serpent, least of all my own."

Pactli stiffened, suddenly upset. He made another gesture, then stalked back across the room without another word.

"Ignore him," Zolin said, turning to leave. "He is a fanatic. Here by his own choice. Come. You will appreciate the next chamber."

Zolin led Cayucali across the central hall and through another passage. It was warmer here. The heat seemed to come from the stones of the Paddock itself. They soon passed from worked stone to natural passages. The air was damp and hot. A large cavern opened suddenly, and the ceiling swooped away above the light of Zolin's candle. Water flowed and splashed in the darkness. The earth beneath Cayucali's bare feet was soft and sandy.

"The baths," Zolin smiled. He handed Cayucali the candle. "You can find your way back to the dormitory?"

Cayucali nodded.

"Good," Zolin said. "Then I will leave you here. You hear the pools. Near them are things for cleaning and drying. Bathe, then sleep. You must rest. I will find you in the morning, when it is time."

Cayucali took a few steps into the cavern. He saw the gleam of dark water and the sheen of firelight dancing on its surface. Steam rose.

"Time?" he repeated. "Time for what?"

"Time to celebrate the liturgy," came Zolin's tired voice. "Time for your first fight. Yax Yapaat has decreed you shall fight under the high sun."

Cayucali turned. A wry smile twisted his rough cheek. Zolin looked sorrowful.

"Is there food?"

"I will show you where, in the morning," Zolin said.

"After I fight, I would like to hear about your tobacco field. To smoke would be most welcome."

"Hard to come by, here in the mountains," Zolin said. He lifted his good arm in a salute, then vanished back through the mouth of the cavern.

Cayucali moved to the edge of the pool. Steam silvered the mirror of the pool, wavering ghostlike in the candlelight. Sweat beaded on his brow and beneath his coarsely woven tunic. He pulled it over his head. Above him, stalactites hung like fat soursop fruits. Water beaded on the lumpy stone and fell in gleaming beads to ripple the shining pool and send the light of the candle dancing through the cave.

He disrobed, then slid into the steaming pool. He stifled a groan as the heat released the dull ache in his bones. The cottony fog in his head cleared, and for the first time he felt free of the stupefying burundanga. He hummed an old song to himself. He laughed at the echoes that crashed around the cave. He let the slight current lift him to the surface of the pool.

Suddenly, his problems seemed clear. He could not stay in

Kalak Mool. If the liturgy did not kill him, that deranged priest would eat his heart in some mad ritual. A poetic end for the exile Cayucali, and Cayucali hated poetry.

But neither could he leave the boy. The Serpent King wanted him for something. Tezca was just young, dumb, and vain enough to believe it would be in his interest. He could not leave Tezca to the Serpent King. And he could not go back to Batun without Tezca. Worse, he needed Tezca willing to speak on his behalf. Clear enough problems, but the solutions remained murky. For the moment, the question was clearer still. Survive tomorrow.

That, he could do.

Blackest Sorcery

When Tezca awoke, his first thought was of home, and how glad he was not to be there. Nightmares plagued him. In each, he explained the reasons the Prince of Tolcalax ordered him back to Batun, and in each, his Master was more upset than in the last. His father sneered. His cousin Uctli mocked him at the Jaguar feast. Tezca bridled at the leftover sensation of shame.

After the feast, Itzamma led him to the luxurious rooms he now occupied. He stretched and yawned under fine linen sheets. Eventually, he dragged himself upright. He pulled on a clean tunic, threw a woolen cape over his shoulder, and walked into the washroom. There, he poured water from a stone ewer into a broad basin and washed his face. The soft carpet beneath his feet brought tears to his eyes. His knees were weak with the suddenness of comfort after weeks—no, months—of deprivation.

The parlor was on the outer edge of the citadel. Along that wall, high windows were open to the sky. Long eaves kept the rain out, and this high on the mountain no insects troubled Kalak Mool. Sunlight, bright and cool, dappled the floors and climbed the walls like flowering vines. High above the emerald valley floor, white cormorants rode warm currents and watched the sapphire lake and the ribbon river that divided the valley. Now and then they folded their wings and dove, their cries carrying on the wind.

Tezca watched them from the tall windows. Absorbed in the pattern, he did not hear Itzamma enter the parlor. The priest's deep, mellifluous voice startled him from his reverie.

"A beautiful sight, is it not?" Itzamma joined him at the window, clasping his hands behind his back. His long, dark hair was pulled back and tied. He stared out over the valley, his eyes sharp and lively. He reminded Tezca of the diving cormorants, or perhaps the black vultures that circled high above.

Tezca nodded. "The rooms are very fine also. Thank you."

Itzamma bowed formally. Then a warm smile cracked his raptor features and he put his hand on Tezca's arm in a fatherly way. "I am glad you approve. I know last night must have been confusing for you. I am sure you have many questions. There are things I would like to discuss with you as well. My private gardens are nearby. Will you join me?"

Tezca lifted his chin and felt the cool morning breeze on his face. The linen tunic was fine, but not warm. It would be warmer in Batun, this time of year. His family was preparing for the season of dances. Uctli said the King might attend. His father was high in the grace of His Eminence. It then occurred to him that whatever he could learn from Yax Yapaat and the High Priest would be of great interest in Batun.

"Show me your gardens," Tezca said. He swung the dyed cloak across his back and followed Itzamma through the doorway into the palace. A short walk along tapestried corridors brought them into the brittle morning sun. Beneath the cloak, Tezca was warm enough. They stood high on the shoulder of the citadel in a small plaza perched at the confluence of several stairways. They passed beneath a stone archway and into a walled courtyard.

Here, the walls blocked the ceaseless wind and caught the warmth of the sun in their stones. Flowering and fruiting espaliers grew so densely against the walls that Tezca could believe himself in the forest. Water murmured; fountains hidden deeper within the gardens melded with birdsong and the hum of bees tumbling from flower to flower. The garden was profuse with a tremendous variety of every plant, root, bulb, and leaf, many of which Tezca recognized as of exquisite rarity. He smiled. Master Tall-Deer would be deeply jealous.

Itzamma led him to a fountain. He seated himself on the rim of the basin and extended his leg as a grimace flashed over his face.

"Would you mind if we sit for a moment?" he asked. "The stairways are steeper than they used to be."

Tezca lifted a broad flower with violet petals in his hand, examining the long stamen. "I have many questions," he said. "But one is more important than the others. Why do you want me to succeed Yax Yapaat? Why does he? Has he no sons, no brothers, no nephews? Is Batun not your enemy? It is difficult to understand."

"Succession is not a matter of blood in Kalak Mool," Itzamma shook his head. "Or it is, but not one of lineages. The Kings of Kalak Mool are avatars. In them dwells a fragment of the divine, a sliver of the Turquoise Serpent himself. This divine fragment is the foundation of the King's authority and the living soul of the Serpent Kingdom. And not every man is suitable to be the vessel of a God."

Tezca was silent. He considered the flower in his hand. A translucent spider crawled across one lavender petal. "What was that, in the ruins?"

"Clever," Itzamma said. "Yes, you sensed the mind of the Turquoise Serpent as he drew near the veil between our world and the world of the Gods. He came to feed on the offering I presented. It is part of the preparation for succession."

"Did he draw me there that night?"

"Who can say?" Itzamma scooped up a handful of pebbles from the basin of the fountain. "Perhaps a necessary confluence. Perhaps something within you wanted to be discovered. But the resonance between you and the Serpent is unmistakable. You are a vessel."

"Are there others?"

"There may be. I know of none. If there were others, I would not be attempting to give the Kingship of Kalak Mool to a son of Batun. Yet the Serpent is not gainsaid. You must be a man of highest breeding." Itzamma flicked his wrist, sending a pebble hurtling toward a lapis kingfisher perched on a dahlia. There was a flash of deep blue against the pale sky, and the bird was gone. "Kalak Mool follows where the Serpent leads. There is much you could accomplish, with the Kingdom at your back. There are many here who yearn for peace with Batun."

Tezca heard Uctli's mocking laughter echo from his dream. "I must think on it more," he said.

"Of course," Itzamma smiled. "For now, we shall talk of simpler things. I understand you are a master of the new sigil-magic. I fear I am hopelessly benighted. Would you speak to me of its rudiments?"

The Anaconda

Cayucali felt an arm on his shoulder. He sat up. The dormitory was quiet around him. True to his word, Zolin stood above him. He lifted his remaining hand to his lips and gestured for Cayucali to follow. Cayucali reached for his ironwood sword, but it was not there.

Zolin led him through the Paddock, through a smoky kitchen, to a long dining room. A yawning servant brought them a bowl of maize porridge mixed with beans and squash and slivers of paca meat. He finished his bowl and the servant brought him another. He finished that one, and the rest of Zolin's too.

"Time remains before your celebration," Zolin said. "What will you do?"

"Is there a shrine where I might pray?"

They abandoned their bowls for the servant. Zolin led them to the long chapel. Within were many shrines, each consecrated to a deity or some aspect of one. At the end of the hall, in the highest place beneath a great stone statue, stood the shrine to the Turquoise Serpent.

Zolin left him in the silence of the chapel. Cayucali walked through the statuary forest, but found no deity there to whom he wished to pray. Instead, the thick burning incense choked him and stung his eyes. The silence and stillness was strained, taut, like the skin of a drum. He felt eyes on the other side of the drumskin. There were minds with foul presences that only waited for the right moment to strike at him.

He left the chapel and made his way back to the training room Zolin showed him the previous night. He took up a restful position against one of the walls and closed his eyes. Perhaps no god would hear his prayer with no shrine to carry his words into the spirit world. But he prayed anyway—he knew not to whom.

"Zolin sent me to find you," a soft voice said.

Cayucali opened his eyes. A fighting man stood above him, tall and lean, with hard muscles that bunched and rolled beneath dark, scarred skin. Cayucali recognized Pactli, the warrior from the night before, and read hostility in his stance.

"It is time for your celebration," Pactli said. "Follow me."

Cayucali stood and followed Pactli through the halls of the Paddock. They came finally to a low room where bright sunlight filled the spaces in a sturdy thornwood gate. The gate led to an arena open to the sky. Zolin stood in the little room. He frowned and spat.

"Time to fight," he said. "When the horn blows."

"Where is my sword?"

"Pactli," Zolin said, "the knife."

Pactli drew a small knife from his belt. It was the stone knife Cayucali had taken from the King's table. He thought it was safe beneath the mattress of his bed in the dormitory. Pactli extended it hilt first toward Cayucali, who ignored it.

"Where is my sword," he said again. "I was promised."

"It is the knife," Zolin said unhappily, "or nothing."

Cayucali took the knife from Pactli, whose expression was smug. Cayucali stared at the short stone blade in his hand. A single note trumpeted from the arena beyond the wooden gate. It echoed against the stone, lingering for long heartbeats. Zolin pushed the gate open. Pactli crossed his arms and blocked the passage back into the Paddock. Cayucali walked out into the sunlight. As he did, he let the blade fall to the floor.

"It is my sword," he said. "Or nothing."

Zolin closed the gate behind him. "Good luck," he said.

The floor of the arena was covered in fine white sand that reflected the sun. He squinted until the glare passed and tensed as he heard the roar of a crowd rise around him. When he could see again, he spun in a slow circle. High stone walls and firm thornwood gates held him fast. The crowd bellowed, but the arena was empty.

Cayucali spun again, shifting his stare from gate to gate, waiting for the threat to emerge. As he turned, the roar of the crowd surged again. There was no movement behind the gates. A flash of color brightened beneath him. His bare foot stirred the white sand, revealing a smear of scarlet.

A flicker of movement pulled at the corner of his eye, but the gates were still. Then he saw it—a slow undulation beneath the sand. The thing arced toward him, nearly invisible beneath the gleaming sand. It came toward him faster and faster now, sloughing the sand from itself in a spray until Cayucali could see it all at once; a great serpent, as long as a ship, wider than the spread of his arms, and thick as a barrel. It had a heavy, blunt snout and dry, shining scales that scintillated in the cool sunlight.

It struck. The blunt snout lifted high, higher than Cayucali could reach with his arms outstretched, then plunged toward him like a hunting hawk. Instinct alone, honed by long years spent in the shadow of death, saved him. He flung himself away from the bludgeoning skull, the flashing fangs, and felt the coarse scrape of scales against skin.

He scrambled to his feet. The serpent had vanished. He swung his head. The tip of its tail burrowed again into the yielding sand. His shoulder bled where the serpent brushed against him. The crowd roared again. He had forgotten them. He heard a coarse whistle and turned to see Zolin kick the little stone knife through the wooden gate. He scowled.

He knew the anaconda's trick now, and marked its languid path in the sand. Even still, the next strike nearly caught him. The great snake seemed to attack from out of the sun. Cayucali leaped aside, and the serpent scraped away another strip of skin. Cayucali raced across the sand to the little stone knife and caught it up just in time to roll away from another strike.

This time, the serpent did not retreat back beneath the soft sand. Instead, it drew itself up again and glared at him with a cold, reptilian eye. He backed slowly away from the wall of the arena. Cayucali readied himself to dive away again, but the serpent seemed content to watch him for the moment. Then he heard the whisper of sand on scales from behind him. It was too late! The dry, muscled body coiled around him.

As the anaconda's body tightened around his chest, he fought to keep his arms free. Each breath felt shallower than the last. He wondered whether he would suffocate, or if the snake would simply crush him. The crowd screamed in delight. Cayucali saw the King, watching from a dais high above the arena.

The serpent's colossal head drew near. Its tongue tasted the air, its head drifted from side to side as it regarded its prey. Cayucali swung his arm viciously. He had only one opportunity. The jaw suddenly gaped wide, revealing cottony pink flesh and rows of pearlescent, curving teeth leading to the dark ring of its throat. The long teeth neared the skin of his shoulder.

Then the knife struck. It plunged through the huge eye and punched through the wall of bone into the creature's brain. Cayucali twisted the blade and ripped it from the wound, dragging it down across the serpent's throat and belly, opening a long and bloody gash in the softer skin. A huge spasm rippled through the monstrous serpent, and Cayucali felt its coils loose for a moment. He clambered out of its embrace as the serpent began to thrash and writhe.

Blood painted the sand, hot and viscous. The howl of the crowd soared even higher. The wooden gates in the walls of the arena opened and men in ritual garments sprinted toward them. Cayucali lifted his knife once again, but the men paid him no heed.

Instead, they knelt in the sand beside the dying serpent and with a strange assortment of stone tools and vessels, collected the bright blood that fell from its mortal wounds. Others collected the very sand beneath the serpent, for it too was soaked in the beast's blood.

He heard a whistle, and saw Zolin gesturing at him to return to the Paddock. Sand clung to the sweat that beaded on his skin under the harsh sun. He touched bruised ribs and groaned. Zolin was silent in the tunnel that lead back to the Paddock, but as Cayucali parted to soak in the baths, Zolin pressed something against his chest. He nodded, and stalked away toward the kitchens.

In the baths, Cayucali unwrapped the waxy leaf and smiled to find three cigars, rolled of fine Kapan tobacco.

A Lesson

In the palace, again in the walled garden, Itzamma drew on stone in chalk. He etched a simple pattern on the flagstones near the fountain where they sat.

"There is a great pleasure in this," the high priest said. "It reminds me of boyhood. It is fitting that as I learn new things, I do so in the same way I learned at my master's feet a lifetime ago."

"Sigilry cannot be entirely new," Tezca said. "Not to one as learned as you?"

"Not entirely, no," Itzamma muttered, his eyes bright in concentration. "The principles are known to me." He completed the pattern and enclosed it with a careful figure of seven sides. "Yet the practical application—ah!"

Itzamma made a sound of delight as he completed the enclosure. A blinding surge of solar energy coalesced through the chalked sigil, like a column of sunlight. Then the stone beneath the chalk sigil splintered with a deafening crack. Itzamma dropped his chalk in surprise, then burst into laughter as a small cloud of dust rose from the cloven flagstone.

Tezca raised his eyebrows. "Impressive, for a novice," he said.

"I have an excellent instructor," Itzamma said. "And I have some skill in other forms of sorcery." He tilted his head and stared at Tezca, his gaze suddenly intense. "Shall I show you? Blood magic cannot be entirely new. Not to one as learned as you."

The high priest's bloody hands, his ferocious eyes, flashed through Tezca's mind. "The principles are known to me," he said.

Itzamma stood. "Then let us turn to a more practical lesson."

He motioned for Tezca to follow him, then strode down an overgrown path, deeper into the garden. In a moment, they came upon a thing half covered in the peach flowers of a creeping trumpet vine, half buried in a bed of tall marigolds. It was a miniature of the palace itself, framed in wood and having many small openings and doors, like a dovecote.

But it did not house doves. Tezca stood at Itzamma's shoulder as the priest opened a small door in the face of the miniature palace. He placed his hand before the dark opening and after a moment, a tiny searching nose emerged from the miniature palace. A tiny gray shrew crept onto Itzamma's hand. It sniffed the air. Itzamma offered the shrew a fat cricket he plucked from another place in the miniature palace. The shrew ate voraciously in Itzamma's palm.

"We are like the shrew," Itzamma said. "Living things and growing things die and putrefy and become soil, that other things may live and grow. The loss of their lives is necessary for the preservation of our lives."

"We are also like the cricket," he continued. "Our lives will yet be ended, our energies taken, by some hungry thing that feeds on us, whether blind crawling worms or jungle cat or—you understand? Action, power, all must come from some source and then become stored in some other source. Nothing is lost. Where would it go?"

"I understand," Tezca said.

Itzamma closed the palace door and walked along the path deeper into the garden, stroking the shrew as it ate. Tezca followed. They came to another small clearing where stood a high stone table.

"The principle is not complex." Itzamma crossed the opening to the far side of the table. The dense garden held the space in silence. The tops of the tallest trees whipped and sawed in the strong wind that never ceased, so high in the mountains as they were, but all around them the garden was still. Even Itzamma's voice seemed muted.

"I can show you the motions, the basic movements," Itzamma said. He pressed the shrew against the stone workbench. A slim stone blade, almost a scalpel, appeared in his other hand. He made three quick incisions, then squeezed the shrew sharply. It seemed to erupt with blood, coating Itzamma's hand and running down his arm. Itzamma dropped the drained carcass of the shrew and turned his arm to allow every drop of blood to coat his skin.

"Coat as much of the skin as you can," he said. "Blood is precious; to waste a drop is a mark of dishonor, and each drop is a well of power." He closed his eyes and clenched his bloody hand into a fist. "The inner motion is far more important. The spark of this cannot be taught. Only developed where it exists. You will sense the vitality of the blood and drink it into yourself. You will know when you have taken in what there is to take."

Before Tezca's eyes, the blood on Itzamma's arm darkened to black. It dried and flaked away like ash. His eyes focused on something infinitely distant. The quiet of the garden glade seemed suddenly deadly.

Itzamma knelt and pressed his hand against the earth beneath his feet. A great pulse shuddered the leaves and vines around him and rattled his bones, and a broad crater appeared at Itzamma's feet. The priest stood and spread his arms.

"Then the power is yours to direct as you wish," he smiled. "Of course, there is much more to it than that, much more. The study of several lifetimes."

Tezca stared at the crater in the earth. He could not help but compare it to the paltry cracked stone his own instructed in sigilry had achieved. Itzamma must have been stifling laughter the entire time. If he could accomplish this with only one tiny shrew...

Itzamma stepped over the crater with alacrity and strode back to the miniature palace. He returned clutching another of the tiny gray shrews. This one struggled and squealed, emitting squeaks at the very threshold of hearing.

"Now," Itzamma said, pressing the squirming shrew into Tezca's palm, "let me show you how."

The Shoreline

※

Cool water lapped against smooth gray stones beneath Cayucali's bare feet. Circling terns screamed overhead. The lakeshore curved away from him, its graceful arc broken by the shapes of other celebrants.

Cayucali walked down the long, narrow wooden trestle out into the deep portions of the lake, where he checked the first of a number of fishing lines set from the end of the trestle. The hook was empty. He placed new bait on the hook and let it sink back down into the water. One of the Blue Knives stood on the shore, watching him carefully as he moved to check the next line.

Down the shore, he recognized another shape in particular; Oahqui, the Commander of the Blue Knives who had captured them in the ruins. Zolin stood near Oahqui, his one arm folded across his chest, observing the labor. Zolin had led the Blue Knives into the dormitory that morning. He announced there were no celebrations scheduled for the day, so they would make themselves useful by helping to bring in the catch, under the strict supervision of Commander Oahqui and the Blue Knives.

Cayucali did not mind. He had grown up fishing for ma-ra and bonefish off the Calaxtin coast. Pulling up robalos on a string was a pleasant enough way to spend a day. And it was a fine day. The blazing sun was warm on his back and the wind was cool on his skin. The lake's water was sweet. Nobody was trying to kill him.

The next line was tense. He bent it with his fingers and felt something pull on the far end of the line. He hauled on it slowly, lifting the line up from the depths. The fish on the end of the line jumped and the line hummed in his hands. It felt like a robalo, and a big one. Then the line went slack, slumping lifelessly in his hands. The tension was gone. He pulled in the line quickly. The fish was gone and the bait with it.

The other lines were more fruitful. He hauled in several fat, blue-green robalos and hefted them into the wicker basket that hung from his shoulders. He baited each line again, then let them sink back into the ponderous abyss. The hook at the end of one line was broken. The gut that bound the hook had frayed; the prong hung loose.

He squatted to bind the hook. He pulled the gut taut around the prong and knotted it carefully, then left the line and hook to dry tight in the warm sun. He smiled as he worked.

Then a shout came across the water. Oahqui stormed over the little wooden paths like a great wave. Zolin followed in his wake. Oahqui pointed, but the wind carried his words away over the face of the lake. Cayucali stood on a small platform at the end of a narrow walkway, far away from the shore. There was nowhere to go, so he waited. Something splashed in the water behind him.

Oahqui arrived with Zolin in tow. He stopped a safe distance from Cayucali and rested his hand on the blade at his side.

"Why do you dawdle? Bait the hook and move to the next," Oahqui said. "What do you plan?"

"Plan?" Cayucali asked. "Not planning. The hook was broken. I fixed it."

"And why would you fix our hook, man of Batun?" he took a menacing step toward Cayucali. "Something smells wrong. I do not believe."

"You do not have to believe," Zolin said to Oahqui. "Celebrant, show us the hook, if you tell us the truth."

Cayucali shrugged. He squatted down to retrieve the bone hook and the drying gut.

The surface of the lake bellowed behind him and a cascade of water soaked his copper skin. Something sinuous and gleaming flashed above his head. It struck the wooden pathway and scrambled past Oahqui quicker than thought. Cayucali glimpsed a thickly muscled torso and webbed skin between broad black claws.

Oahqui regained his poise instantly. He drew his knife and began to turn to face the creature even as it slithered around him, cracking the wooden boards of the pathway beneath it as it went. Oahqui stabbed at the creature but it was already past.

It slammed into Zolin without hesitation, wrapping its short, thick limbs around him and carrying him off the pathway. They broke the silvery surface of the lake with a second splash. The creature's long tail thrashed once, twice, churning the blue water into a sparkling foam. Then they were gone.

Oahqui turned back to Cayucali. "Some part of your scheme, I do not doubt." His blade hung loosely at his side as he took a subtle step toward Cayucali. "I was the real target, was I not?"

Cayucali watched Oahqui's eyes. They ignored the long knife carefully. Cayucali lifted his hands and took his own step backward. He teetered on the edge of the walkway.

"Not my doing, Commander," Cayucali said. "I was just fixing the hook."

"I find that very difficult to believe," Oahqui said. His voice was empty. He took another small step toward Cayucali.

"It is a Salamander," Cayucali said. "A hunter. Let me go after it. I can rescue Zolin, but I must be quick."

Oahqui laughed. "I know what it was, and I know Zolin is not coming back. As I would not come back, if you had your way." He gestured with the blade. "Back to the shore. Now."

Cayucali glanced down the long, precarious pathway that led back to the shore. The shore converged with the horizon itself, and the pathway seemed to vanish against that distant line. Oahqui stood athwart the wooden planks, his blade back at his side, a deadly stillness in his face. Cayucali would have to squeeze past him, to put his back to the Blue Knife to get back to the shore. He did not like the idea of that. And Zolin did not have much time.

He felt the far edge of the pathway with his heel. He let the basket of robalos fall from his shoulders. Oahqui saw his intent in a moment and lunged toward him with the blade. But it was too late. Cayucali leapt backward, twisting and arching in the air, then pierced the cool water like a thrown spear.

The Aviary

Xhoc led Tezca deep into the mountain. They passed rich suites of salons, libraries, kitchens, gardens, fountains, and all the finery of the palace. The palace guards bowed to her as they passed, and Tezca found their bows appropriate. Xhoc was beautiful and pleasant; an aura of peace and dignity surrounded her. She received these gestures with amusement and an easy grace that left each man pleased to have offered his respect.

At the end of the long and twisting hall, just as Tezca was beginning to wonder how there could be an aviary under so much stone, they came to a latticed gate. Sunlight and fresh air poured through the lattice. Tezca heard the sound of birdsong beyond the gate. They had come through the mountain so quickly! Xhoc pushed, and the gate swung open easily.

"Is there a second sun? A sun inside the earth itself?" Tezca wondered.

Xhoc laughed. "Perhaps, but we have not gone that deep. A high and hidden valley only. We have not come all the way through the mountain. The aviary is home to many birds, because few things but birds can find their way here."

"Itzamma says a condor nests here," Tezca said. "He needs a tailfeather."

"I have heard so," Xhoc said, "though I do not know where the condor nests, except roughly. Only the Royal Household and its guests may enter the aviary, but since the Royal Household of Yax Yapaat is only me and a few old cousins, I will guide you as best I can. I have not been here since I was a girl. But Itzamma would not send us on a fool's errand. I'm sure we will find the condor's nest quickly. Why does he need the tailfeather?"

"It is part of the ritual of coalescence," Tezca said. "He says the condor's blessing is essential."

"Oh," the princess said, suddenly disinterested. "Of course."

The silence lingered. Tezca cursed himself for his blunt response.

"Is there no other way into the valley?" he tried.

Xhoc was gracious. Her tone became kind again. "There is, though I have never seen it. South of here, they say, is a vast and trackless wilderness. They say the condor nests near there, somewhere, but it is full of deadly things, and wicked lawless people who hate both Kalak and Batun alike."

"Master Tall Deer says the world ends in the far south. It grows thinner and thinner until there is nothing at all."

"Here, the wise say that there is a great kingdom beyond the wilderness, the kingdom of the Gods of the Sun, which they name Chimor."

Tezca shrugged. "Until a week ago, Kalak Mool was only a fable to the south. Why should Chimor not lie beyond?"

Around them, the air was alive with movement. Gemstone hummingbirds sipped from rainbow-flowered trumpet vines and aramacas screeched from the canopy above them, flashes of bloodred among the endless verdant green. A well-kept stone path led them past flowering bushes and tall trees laden with fruits. A keel-billed toucan slashed at star apples and fluttered its black wings indignantly at a caretaker who toiled among the bushes to the side of the path.

"Do you think us savages?" Xhoc asked. "Your people sought to destroy us. It was not so long ago."

"I never thought of you at all," Tezca said, then cursed himself again. "I mean, no one ever spoke of Kalak Mool in Batun. I knew there was a war before I was born, but the details were never relevant to me. Master Tall Deer thought it settled and done. I never thought you savages. No city of savages could cultivate such a beautiful garden."

"And the thing you saw in the ruins? The thing Itzamma did?" Xhoc asked.

They walked deeper into the aviary for some time before he answered. Birdsong surrounded them now, and the emerald arms of the jungle kept the high mountain wind from them, so they grew warm. Tezca threw his cloak over his shoulder. Xhoc stopped to peer at a giant mantis perched on the sunlit apex of the branch of a flowering alatze tree.

"It scared me," Tezca said, "and fascinated me. I confess, I am still of two minds. But Itzamma is a fine teacher. Under his instruction, I can see that Batun's disagreement with Kalak Mool may be only one of perspective. Men like him are perhaps above such petty squabbling."

Xhoc nodded, still staring at the mantis. "Itzamma is a learned man. He has been our high priest as long as I can recall. His power is very great. I am sure you will profit under his tutelage."

Tezca smiled. His chest swelled. He filled his lungs with the sweet and living air of the aviary and the intoxicating perfume of Xhoc's approval, as it seemed to him. She turned away from the mantis and they continued down the path.

"We must leave the trees," Xhoc said, "we must see the sky."

They followed the slope of the valley up into the shoulders of the high peaks as the sun climbed high in the sky and banished the shadows. Above them, fat and woolly rams leapt and played on bare stone slopes too steep for soil to settle. A narrow path led them abreast of the forest canopy, where colorfully-feathered motmots and trogons hunted and played among the highest leaves.

"Too bad another tailfeather would not work as well," Xhoc said. "We could have our pick."

Tezca stared into the sky and saw something vast pass across the face of the sun. He pointed. "What is that?"

Xhoc craned her neck. "I cannot see it," she said.

"There—in the sun," he said.

She stared another moment, then cried out in delight. "The condor! Flying south—to nest. We must follow!"

She began to trot down the narrow path, the bronze skin of her strong legs flashing through the slits in her tunic. The iridescent quetzal feathers in her hair, markers of her royal status, fluttered with each fall of her foot as though still animated by the spirit of the bird. Her gaze was rapt to the condor high above and she did not look back. After a moment, he grinned and followed after her.

The Salamander

Cayucali claimed one final gasp of the sweet mountain air before he disappeared beneath the surface. Bubbles and foam exploded around him as he crashed into the warm lake. As his eyes adjusted and the water grew clear, he spotted the Salamander. Despite the powerful sweeping of its muscular tail, it moved slowly and awkwardly through the limpid water. Zolin was not a small man. Though he had only one arm, his desperate thrashing made him a difficult burden.

Cayucali dove after them. Zolin's thrashing would only cost him precious breath. The Salamander clamped its massive jaws around Zolin's shoulder. No amount of thrashing would break that vice grip bite. Cayucali had seen the shy, fierce salamander only a few times before. On one occasion, the river-dwelling beast locked its jaws around a girl's leg. Six strong men failed to pry its jaws apart. Yet only Zolin's thrashing kept the Salamander from vanishing swiftly into some hidden den. Struggling had saved him, but could now cost him his life.

Cayucali could see the beast's den now. The salamander made for a rocky outcropping that thrust upward from the lakebed far below and neared the sunlit surface. It looked like a mountain hidden beneath the water. The salamander vanished into a small opening shrouded by plants that grew thickly toward the sunlight. Cayucali pushed aside thick root tendrils of hyacinth and waterlily and pulled himself into the belly of the stone.

His chest pounded and ached. His eyes strained against the darkness of the passage. His thick hands scrabbled against the moss-covered ceiling of the passage until he burst into a pocket of stale air. He dragged himself out of the water and collapsed amid a scatter of pale bones, barely illuminated by the dim and hazy light that filtered through the water passage. Deeper in the cave, he heard Zolin groaning. A splash, then silence.

He sprinted across the mound of bones, which scattered and splintered beneath his feet, and into another pool on the far side of the cavern. The salamander had chosen its den well, but had grown too ambitious with its prey. Zolin was not a young man, but still fought with surprising vigor. He must have been a strong man in his own day.

Cayucali caught the beast just as it dragged Zolin beneath the water once again. He clamped his arms around the salamander's belly and dragged it deeper still into the pool. Its skin felt eerily human; scaleless and clammy. Weightless in the water, Cayucali pressed his hips to the creature and locked his legs around it. It thrashed wildly, but kept its jaws clamped to Zolin's chest. Small, sharp teeth punctured the old man's skin. Blood darkened the water.

Cayucali crawled his hands to the salamander's head and found its gills. He clapped his palms across the tender frills and pressed them into the salamander's head as tightly as he could. The beast spasmed, thrashing harder than ever, but Cayucali wrapped one leg over the other and squeezed tighter still. Finally, the salamander's instincts overruled its hunger. It opened its mouth, and Zolin floated free.

Cayucali released the salamander. With a vicious twist of its tail, it disappeared into the darkness of the pool. His own chest burned with the need for a breath. Cayucali dragged Zolin back into the air pocket and blew into his mouth until he spat up two lungfuls of lakewater. Zolin tried to sit up, but Cayucali told him to rest. He pressed his hands to the semi-circular wound on Zolin's shoulder. The salamander's bite was not deep. Its bite held no venom. The blood flow quickly stopped. After a few moments, his breathing steadied and his eyes fluttered open.

"Thanks for coming after me," Zolin gasped.

"Least I could do to pay you back for the tobacco," Cayucali said. "Did you save any strength for the swim back? That salamander will not stay away long."

Zolin stuck out his good arm and Cayucali pulled him to his feet. Then, after picking their way across the mound of bones, they began the long, slow swim back to the shore.

As they trudged up the beach, soaking and exhausted, they were met by a bristling hedge of blades wielded by a cohort of Blue Knives. Oahqui stood at their head, wearing a grim frown.

"Commander, what—"

Oahqui's backhanded blow cracked across Zolin's jaw like a chisel splitting stone. The older man staggered back, nearly falling into the lake again before he caught himself.

"Bind the prisoner," Oahqui said. He gestured, and the Blue Knives surged forward like jaguars. They seized Cayucali and lashed his wrists once again. They pushed him down, driving him into the pebbled stones of the beach. Zolin stepped toward Cayucali, but Oahqui threw out a hand in warning.

"One more step," he said, "and I will name you an accomplice."

"Accomplice?" Zolin cried, "to what?"

"He thinks the salamander is part of some plot," Cayucali sneered.

Oahqui placed a sandal on the back of his neck and bent down toward Cayucali. "I do think so," he said. "And though it is more than you deserve, I will make my accusation formally. I will permit a Magistrate to decide the matter. You are part of the liturgy, after all."

He made another gesture to the Blue Knives. They dragged Cayucali to his feet and surrounded him, shoving him down the path that led toward the city. One among them began to call loudly in phrases Cayucali did not recognize, but had the ring of ritual.

As he passed Zolin, the old master of the Paddock caught his eye and looked ashamed.

"Cayucali," he said, "I am sorry."

Cayucali only shrugged. One of the Blue Knives kicked him from behind. He offered the old man a quick smile before stumbling past.

"Find me some more tobacco!" he shouted.

The Condor

Tezca and Xhoc left the aviary as the sun peaked in the sky. The forest canopy was a sea of jade leaves just beneath them as they came to the end of the hidden valley. The shoulders of the mountains rolled under their feet and skittish rams bleated indignantly at the invasion of their territory. The condor had vanished over the ridge where they now stood. They peered into the wilderness beyond.

"Can we get down there?" Xhoc asked. "It is so steep."

"Look," Tezca said, pointing. "Like you said. There is a path. Hard to see."

"I see it," Xhoc said, tightening her sandals. "You go first."

Tezca found the trailhead and began the long descent into the lowlands south of Kalak Mool. Midway down the face of the slope, Xhoc shouted. He spun, then followed his finger with his eyes. The condor, which had been circling further to the south, now plunged beneath the line of the trees. A distant, titanic scream echoed across the lowlands. Xhoc gave him a radiant smile, and he returned it with one of his own.

"Did you see where it came down?" Xhoc pressed her

quetzal feathers against her head to keep the wind from lashing them against her face.

"Near the cliffs," Tezca said. "Not too far."

At the bottom of the slope, Tezca turned to look at the way they had come. The path disappeared into the charcoal stone of the slope, buried in the tufts of tall, yellowing grass. Despite having climbed down that slope only moments before, he could not trace the way they had come.

Though they had left the aviary itself, the sound of birdsong was not less. The lands south of Kalak Mool were lower, warmer, wetter. The warm hum of insects filled the shadowed eaves of the jungle that fringed the slope. They followed the fringe of dense jungle southwest, toward the place they had last seen the condor. The sun was hotter here, a constant presence on their shoulders. They walked in the shade of the trees, swatting at the fat black flies that swarmed them from deeper in the forest.

The fringe of shadow grew as Tezca and Xhoc came to the foot of the stony hill. No hidden path necklaced this hill, no secret way made the ascent any easier.

"Is the nest there?" Xhoc asked.

Tezca squinted into the sky. He could see nothing above him but the blue span of the sky and the golden orb of the sun sinking west.

"I see nothing," he said. "But that means nothing."

"Maybe there is a feather on the ground," Xhoc said.

They searched the earth at the foot of the hill for a time, but Tezca was quickly forced to admit that the smallish feathers he found in the dust were not the tailfeathers of the great bird he had seen earlier.

"It must be up there," he said. "It must be."

Xhoc crossed her arms over her chest as she stared up the escarpment and made a skeptical face.

"You could fall to your death," she said.

Tezca nodded. "Then you climb."

Xhoc shook her head. "This is your task. You are the vessel. Besides that, you're a man. Your arms are longer. And stronger—I hope."

Tezca found grips in the harsh stone and planted his sandaled foot on a spray of coarse orange lichen and pulled himself upward, toward the next desperate handhold. This, he repeated so many times he lost count. Once, he craned his head around to try to look down at Xhoc. His stomach turned and his vision echoed with memories of the nightmare storm that had brought him to Kalak Mool. The memory of pain seared through the bones of his arms. He nearly lost his grip on the steep stone face.

But he did not fall. He climbed on. After a time, he came to a lip of stone. The vertical face of the cliff continued to rise above him, but he breathed a long, trembling sigh. A ledge. A place to rest. He dragged himself over the lip and collapsed on the swathes of tough grasses that grew there. His breath rasped in his chest and he turned his face to the setting sun for a few blissful moments of rest. Then he pulled himself to the edge and looked down to where he hoped Xhoc still waited.

She stood at the base of the cliff, craning her pale face up toward him and waving her arms broadly. She cupped her hands around her mouth and shouted something up to him, but the wind tore her words and he could not make them out.

The tough grass left spiny burrs clinging to the fine cloth of his tunic. He sat up and tried to brush the burrs away. Something moved in the corner of his eye, and there was a monstrous creaking sound, as of some colossal hinge turning. Tezca turned his head. To his left, the ledge widened. Built in a pocket of stone where the ledge met the cliff face was a massive nest, constructed of bent branches and the collected detritus of the jungle.

The condor stared at Tezca from the nest. He heard the

creaking sound again as the condor unfolded massive wings and settled them again.

The beast glittered in the sinking sunlight. Gold baubles and silver fetishes dangled and clanked among glistening black feathers, chiming in the soft wind. A sinuous pink neck, girdled in jeweled gold bands, supported its raptor head. It peered at him with vermillion pupils over a hooked beak bleached bonewhite by the sun. It was taller than him without standing.

Tezca tensed, stepping away from the condor. He could not survive a leap from the ledge. But the condor only regarded him. Something in its gaze put him at ease, and he suddenly felt sure it was no threat to him. He moved toward the nest. Its small, yellow eyes were intelligent. As he drew near, the condor's head snaked forward until they were face to face. Something passed between them, and the condor dipped its great head in acknowledgment.

Then it curled its head around itself and plucked a single long feather from its tail and presented it to Tezca. The thick spine of the feather was as long as his leg and coated in some fragrant oil. Tezca stared at the condor for another long moment.

He made a bow, then took the feather from the condor. Within its maw glinted sharp teeth, all capped with yet more gold, set with fined and faceted gems. Tezca snatched his hand away. The condor seemed amused. It shook itself again, spreading radiant wings and sending forth a wave of golden chimes.

It leapt from the ledge in a single, powerful motion, lifting itself into the sky with a pulse of vast, shimmering wings. A single, piercing scream nearly deafened him. Then it was gone, a dark mote fading toward the horizon.

Judgment

In the fields that surrounded the citadel of Kalak Mool, the life of the city played out in slow rhythms. Smallholders tended fields encircled by low stone walls and planted densely with tangled crop gardens. Maize plants grew beneath tall guava and cacao trees. Vines heavy with bean pods wound round their stems and the understory was planted thick with pink-flowering achiote and fragrant vanilla.

Children drove mixed herds of goats and pigs through the fields, and chased particolored chickens through the undergrowth. Laborers dragged stone from the quarry on sleds that moved through slotted paths. A team of builders shaped and fitted stones to repair a tall storage silo beside the path that led from the lake to the citadel.

Commander Oahqui and his serpent guard led Cayucali along that path. The children stopped to watch, spurred back into motion only when one of their goats strayed too far. The late afternoon sun stretched the shadows of the surrounding peaks across the valley. Where the sliding shadows touched, labor ceased; men, women, children, and animals all began to return to the citadel.

The column came to a place where another road crossed theirs. Oahqui signaled a halt. The shadows stretched longer, lengthening across the road and shrouding Cayucali in the cooler air of evening. The tenor of the birdsong in the valley changed. The bright calls of macaws and terns faded to the soft coos of mourning doves. Green moths as large as his open hand rose from the grass and tumbled from flower to flower. Men sat along the edge of the road, talking quietly or casting dice.

Finally, Oahqui grunted in satisfaction. He stood, and gestured for the column to follow. A lonely figure wandered along the other road toward the crossing. A staff rested across his shoulder. From it, a burning lantern swung. It cast a yellow pool of light around the wanderer's feet. It wavered and pulsed with each step and marked him clearly in the gathering dusk.

The Blue Knives pushed Cayucali to the front until he stood beside Oahqui, who raised his hand toward the approaching figure.

"Magistrate!" he said. "I demand judgment."

The figure stopped. The lantern's swaying slowed.

"Who does?" came the reply.

"I, Oahqui, Commander of the Blue Knives, demand judgment."

The magistrate shifted his weight to his other foot. He was short, stocky, long-bearded, shrouded in a banded cotton cloak, and bore a large pack across his shoulders.

"Against whom?" he asked.

"Against this man," Oahqui pulled Cayucali forward. "A celebrant of the Liturgy of Coalescence."

"Very well," the magistrate said. "Arrange your men here. You, the accuser, shall stand there. You," he said, pointing to Cayucali, "stand over there and prepare to make your statement."

The magistrate carried no weapon other than his ceremonial staff. He spoke with supreme confidence, full of the expectation of obedience.

"Commander Oahqui—when I say so, you shall stand beside the lantern and make your accusation. Then the accused shall make his answer in the same manner. Then I shall ask any questions I have. Having answered these, I will render my judgment, which may not be gainsaid by any but His Highness."

He thrust his staff into the soft earth beside the path and let his pack fall from his shoulders. In the blink of an eye, he had arranged a high-backed chair and a slim writing desk on the ground beside the path. He lit another small lantern and hung it from one side of his seat so that it spilled its light over his desk. He placed a broad-brimmed hat on his head and seated himself on the high-backed chair, then waved his arm broadly. While the magistrate prepared, spectators gathered in the gloom beyond the circle of firelight. Cayucali had an audience.

"Commander Oahqui, when you are ready, you may make your accusation."

Oahqui stood proudly beside the staff, bathed in the golden light of the lantern. The candle inside was made of some fragrant resin that repelled the clouds of light-hungry insects.

"Magistrate, this man is a celebrant in the great rite of the Serpent. Because there were no celebrations scheduled for today, he, along with others, were tasked with aiding our fishermen in bringing in their catch from the lake. A malcontent, dismissive of our charity, he lured me out into the lake, where he caused a salamander to attack me that he might flee his obligation to the Serpent.

"I defended myself against the beast, who took Zolin the Paddockmaster instead. This one attempted his escape anyway, disobeying my command to return to the shore and diving into the lake in an act of cowardice. He came ashore some distance away, and only by the vigilance of the Blue Knives was he recaptured. His actions would have disrupted the Liturgy of Coalescence! The punishment is death!"

The magistrate made certain notes behind his desk, then steepled his fingers and leaned forward.

"Thank you, Commander," he said. "The accused shall now make his answer."

Cayucali took Oahqui's place in the lantern's glow. The sky was dark now, the sun a smear of distant flame far behind the great peaks of the mountains that pierced the heavens like the points of spears. He bowed to the magistrate.

"Some of what Oahqui said was true. I am a prisoner, forced to participate in your rites. I spent the day checking fishing lines. But I made no plan to escape, no deal with the salamander. A salamander does not have the wits to make agreements with men."

"Then he is a sorcerer! A practitioner of forbidden arts, having truck with—" Oahqui snapped.

The magistrate waved a hand. "The accuser shall remain silent or be censured."

Oahqui glowered.

Cayucali continued. "The salamander attacked Zolin. It took him into the lake. I followed, because Zolin showed me kindness in the Paddock. In the salamander's lair, I drove the creature away from Zolin. We returned to the shore because it was the only place to go. Commander Oahqui jumps at shadows."

"Are there any witnesses to these things?"

"Magistrate, my entire divison witnessed these things," Oahqui said, waving his hand at the column of Blue Knives.

The Magistrate raised an eyebrow. "Is this not *your* division, loyal to you? How can I trust what they will tell me? No, I wish to hear from the Paddockmaster. Is he here?"

After a few moments, Zolin stepped forward. "I am here, magistrate."

"Good," the magistrate said, steepling his fingers and regarding Zolin over his hands. "I am glad you are hale. Give me your oath and tell me—what happened?"

Zolin rubbed his head with his good hand. "It is difficult to recall, but I swear to tell you the truth."

"Did the celebrant rescue you?"

"He did," Zolin said.

"Did he rescue *you*, or did he help you as part of his attempt to escape?"

"The salamander dragged me to its nest, in a cave beneath the lake. No. How could that be part of an escape?"

"Is it true you showed the celebrant kindness in the Paddock?"

"It is true," Zolin said. "A small kindess. He wished to smoke, so I gave him cigars."

The magistrate nodded. "Very well. Thank you, Paddockmaster. I have heard what I need to hear. I will now render my decision. Accuser, accused, step forth. Stand in the light."

When Cayucali and Oahqui stood in the glow of the lantern, the Magistrate spoke again. "First, I find that the celebrant disobeyed a rightful command from one with authority to give it.

"Only to rescue Zolin," Cayucali said. "He commanded me to let Zolin die!"

"Yet Commander Oahqui has authority over you," the magistrate asked. "And did you not disobey him? To ignore this is to ignore justice."

Oahqui grinned. Cayucali felt a moment of fury toward Oahqui, an uncharacteristic vindictiveness. He let it go with a long breath.

"Nevertheless," the magistrate said. He leaned back in his seat. "I do not find that the accused created any scheme or plot, or had any agreement with the salamander. Therefore, the punishment of death is not warranted."

The magistrate continued. "The accused did what he did

for a noble purpose; our justice must account for this. In addition, he is a celebrant and of great importance to His Highness. Therefore his sentence shall be the lesser."

The magistrate cleared his throat and his sentence rolled from his lips like crashing waves. Beyond the firelight, those gathered to observe leaned forward in excitement.

"All you men and spirits who hear my words bear witness to my judgment. On the morning before his next celebration, the accused's shoulders and hips shall be dislocated by the drawing-rope."

"Then, he shall celebrate the liturgy. Such is my judgment."

Then he dimmed his lantern, packed his things, and went upon his way.

The Way Back

Tezca pressed his hand against his thin cloak for the hundredth time. The condor's feather was still there. The night was cold, his cloak insufficient. Mist rose in the forest. Tezca did not know how they had come to be in the forest, but they had. They had lost the fringe they followed from the aviary to the condor's nest. As he touched the feather beneath his cloak again, he admitted they had lost the aviary itself.

"This was a mistake," Xhoc said, from beside him. "We should never have entered the forest. No one goes into the forest at night. It is the domain of monstrous things. Even children know this."

The night hummed with the sound of frogs chirping, insects buzzing, and the skitter of small things hunting in the brush.

"It was not by choice," Tezca muttered.

"Something follows us," Xhoc said.

"Nothing follows us," Tezca said.

But something followed them. He heard it in the trees behind them; leaves rustled when no breeze blew, and red eyes reflected moonlight when the canopy of trees opened above them. Too many eyes, too far apart. Whatever followed them, there was more than one. Wherever Tezca led them, the things followed, never lagging far behind, never drawing too close. He thought he saw one once: a man-sized shape, dark and ungainly, scrambling along a branch high above.

"We are lost," Xhoc said. "We must go north. If I could only see the stars..."

"There is one thing I could try," Tezca said. "Though I have never tried before."

When they came to the next break in the tree canopy, where moonlight filtered through in long silver beams and scattered pale light on the soft forest floor, Tezca stopped. He knelt on the ground and rooted through the soft layer of rotting leaves. Sweet-smelling loam crumbled in his hands and stained his fingernails black. Earthworms wound around his fingers and curled like sea-dragons as they sought the comforting warmth of the soil.

Something white gleamed in the mulch. He snatched the grub from the rotting leaves and stood. The fat, white beetle grub filled the palm of his hand with a surprising weight. He stared at it for a moment, trying to recall what Itzamma showed him in the palace garden. He closed his fist. The beetle grub squirmed, then burst in his hand. Thick juices oozed between his fingers and down over the back of his wrist.

Tezca closed his eyes. He cast his mind through the night and sought the glow of strength he released from the beetle grub. It was an unfamiliar motion of the spirit. Nothing in the sigilry he learned from Master Tall Deer prepared him to flail around this unfamiliar space. The sigils were lenses, and only required him to direct his awareness into the sigil itself. They created patterns, labyrinths that ordered untrammeled reality.

Blood sorcery was different. There was no sigil, no pattern. There was only the wilderness of the reality, full of spirit and the energies that underlied the paltry world visible seen by men. To navigate that wilderness demanded an act of will. Tezca let the purity of his desire to escape whatever hunted him sharpen his questing thought to a razor edge.

He found the essence of the beetle grub even as he let its crushed carcass fall from his hand. He seized hold of it like a jaguar fishing a robalo from a river, sinking claws through taut skin. He swallowed it and it became a part of him, suffusing him and adding to his own strength, which he suddenly felt as a well of bright, warm water.

Xhoc gasped. A dimly pulsing light came from Tezca's hand. Something stirred in the branches above them.

Tezca closed his eyes again. He formed his intention again, fixed the latticed thornwood gate to the aviary firmly in his mind. Something had shifted in him during the climb to the condor's nest, and when that wise beast's eyes met his. He had claimed the tail feather, and Itzamma would be proud. It was a kingly deed. Not even that oafish warrior Cayucali could dispute him.

He smiled. Cayucali would like what came next even less. He formed a channel from the well within himself and power flowed through it. In the moonlit glade, an orb of smoky light coalesced in front of him. It swirled and effervesced like a living thing. It cast a greenish light on the boles of trees around them. A tarantula squeezed itself into a hole in the wood. Xhoc drew her cloak tighter around herself.

"You made it?" she asked. "What is it?"

The orb shuddered, then began to drift across the clearing toward the opposing wall of trees.

"I think we are meant to follow it," he said.

"You are not certain?"

Tezca flushed. "I am certain," he said. "We follow it." He stalked forward after the orb, and Xhoc followed.

"Itzamma says I am the most gifted pupil he has ever taught," Tezca said. "He says I will be a great king."

"I am sure you will be," Xhoc said. "The way you treated the beetle grub showed you know what it means to be King."

They drifted into silence as they followed the smoking orb. Whatever followed them seemed hesitant of the light and fell further behind into the dark jungle. They abandoned the chase altogether as Tezca and Xhoc came to the edge of the forest and emerged into the bright moonlight. Before them was the hidden path that climbed to the aviary. They shared a smile, then began the climb.

Countrymen

※

Dawn came, driving high thin clouds across the vault of the sky and bathing the citadel of Kalak Mool in a strange, granular light. In the dormitory buried deep within the mountain, Cayucali knew morning had come, and with it the time for another celebration. The taciturn warrior Pactli was dawn's harbinger. He came for Cayucali and brought him to Zolin, who again managed the Paddock's affairs from the sunlit mouth of the long corridor.

As Cayucali followed Pactli toward the gate to the arena, he saw a cohort of servitors come through the distant gate bearing some burden. In another moment, he recognized it as a hewn and mangled corpse. Pactli swung his head heavily.

"You knew him?"

"I knew him," Pactli said. "I thought better of him."

When they came to the gate, Zolin ordered it opened. The day's strange light shone on him. In the center of the arena, several men stood around a wooden device. Cayucali recognized one of them as the Magistrate. Zolin's hand fell on his shoulder.

"What you did for me in the lake, I cannot repay. Not

with any amount of tobacco. I am an old man now, crippled, a willing slave of my own enemies. But I still love my life."

Pactli sneered.

"We do not all share your great faith," Zolin said to Pactli. To Cayucali, he said, "Oahqui awaits you, as does the Magistrate. I fear you have made an enemy of the first. But I gave my testimony to the Magistrate. I hope it will help."

"Thank you, Zolin," Cayucali said.

Pactli led him through the gate and toward the device in the center of the arena. The white sand was cool on his feet.

"No knife this time?" Cayucali asked.

"The great man is great without a weapon," Pactli said.

"The great man is made great more by how he lives than by how he dies."

Pactli sneered again. "Only one path remains open to us."

Oahqui and the Magistrate watched them approach. As they did, the Blue Knives coiled loops of coarse rope around his wrists and threw the rope over a complex pulley high on the wooden device.

"Celebrant," the magistrate intoned, "your arms and legs are to be dislocated from your body as punishment for your wrongful disobedience."

He nodded to the Blue Knives, who pulled the ropes taut. Cayucali was dragged against the wooden device. More ropes coiled around his ankles. His body was bent like a bow. An incredible pressure filled his arms and legs.

In reflex, he strained against the ropes, but even his tremendous strength could not resist the cunning leverages created by the pulleys and the ropes. The pressure increased, and moved to dwell his shoulders and his hips. It built to a climax, bending his joints until he felt he must be torn apart. The arena was hushed, listening. A sharp crack echoed across the stone enclosure, then another. His left shoulder went first, then his right. Then a third crack, a double sound and louder than the others, marked his hips giving way.

There was a moment of relief as the pressure ceased. Then the pain hit him. It radiated through his limbs like a fire. He could not catch himself as the Blue Knives released the ropes. He fell into the fine sand, turning his face so he could breathe. The Blue Knives dismantled the device and disappeared into another gate from the arena.

Oahqui squatted beside him and smiled. "You are a stubborn man. Why did you refuse to cry out? You made me lower myself to see your tears." He stood, and kicked sand in Cayucali's face. "I know you will not learn your lesson, but I don't think that matters any more." He followed the Blue Knives out of the arena.

Cayucali heard footfalls in the soft sand beside him. The Magistrate's stern voice reached him.

"Your debt is paid," he said. "My judgment is satisfied in every respect—except one."

Something crashed into the sand beside him.

"The liturgy is not served by the death of a helpless lamb. The justice and integrity of the ritual requires me to grant you this judgment. I have heard that you were deprived of your sword. I amend my judgment accordingly."

Now the footsteps moved away

"Now you must acquit yourself," the magistrate said, from afar. "Die well, warrior." Then he too was gone from the arena.

In his place, three men entered from a gate in the far side of the arena wall. They bore crude wooden blades and ragged scraps of armor. Fear drove him to action. He rolled to one side and groaned as bone ground against bone. His left shoulder and hip clicked back into place with a sickening crunch and a spike of agony. He pushed himself to the other side and felt his right hip fall into place.

The men came forward. Cayucali gathered his legs beneath him and came to his knees. His right arm hung limp, his right shoulder burned. The three stalked across the sand, raising their swords. By their motions, they were not warriors. Yet something about them was familiar. Something in the cast of their jaws, the lines of their noses.

With his left hand, he dug in the sand for the thing the Magistrate had left. His fingers closed around a leather-bound hilt, and he knew it for what it was. His sword.

Then the men were upon him. One came forward quickly, raising crude sword high. Cayucali leapt away, diving out from beneath the falling blade. As he struck the sand and rolled, his shoulder fell into place with an agonizing shock. His arms trembled as he lifted the ironwood blade toward his attackers. His legs shook as he circled, keeping them all in sight. His blade dropped for a moment. He knew them. They were his countrymen. They were Tolcalaxtin, like him.

They howled in rage driven by great fear, then charged. He banished the pain and weariness from his weakened limbs and raised his blade against men of his homeland.

Afterward, as blood purpled the sand in the morning's cruel cloudlight, the masked priests rushed into the arena with their scoops and receptacles to a rich harvest. A horn blew, and Cayucali turned to see a fine procession make its way into the arena. Among the train of clean, beautiful faces he saw the King, Yax Yapaat—and beside him the young wizard, Tezca.

The Warning

Tezca looked for Xhoc, but she had vanished. He was alone in the company of Yax Yapaat and the royal court. Far below, in the arena, the warlord Cayucali made quick work of the three other men despite his horrifying injuries. He found himself pleased when the last man collapsed beneath the edge of the Cayucali's blade. He told himself it was only because the liturgy and his coronation depended on successful celebrations.

Around him, vulpine faces stared eagerly into the arena. A flutter of excitement moved through the court as the celebration concluded, and Yax Yapaat was prevailed upon to lead the court into the arena to grace the celebrant with a congratulatory audience. The court agreed that visiting the arena floor, where Itzamma's collectors separated sacred blood from sand, would be a diverting affair.

So Tezca came to stand in the arena, where the sun, which now burned away some of the high flat clouds, illuminated the white sand into a blinding mirror. Above it, Cayucali stood like a stone pillar. His ironwood blade hung from one hand. The royal procession halted, and servants deployed shades and waved fans woven of bright plumage to cool the illustrious gathered there. Watchful Blue Knives, members of the King's guard, imposed themselves between the prisoner and the royal procession.

"Warrior," said the herald of Yax Yapaat, "the King found your performance most stirring. You have honored this liturgy. Xicuoatl will be pleased."

Cayucali said nothing.

Tezca frowned. The stubborn old fool. To show disrespect to Yax Yapaat was to show disrespect to him. Did Cayucali not know that Tezca was the vessel? That he was destined to ascend the Waterlily Throne? Cayucali simply stared at him, silent as the eager nobility chattered around them. Tezca's face flushed at the idiocy of the simpering courtiers around him. When he was King...

The King's guard forced Cayucali to his knees. Tezca smirked. The old warrior was so haughty only nights ago, when it was Tezca who fell to his knees. He acted so superior, coming back to save him from the Blue Knives. Tezca had almost thanked him then, but he knew the truth now. Cayucali was simply jealous of Tezca's elevation, ashamed of his own fall from King Chimal's favor. Tezca had almost allowed the oaf to deprive him of his destiny. But the world had changed.

Yax Yapaat touched Tezca's elbow. Tezca followed him forward, through the milling courtiers, until only bare white sand stood between them and Cayucali. In the distance, priests hunched around the motionless forms of the other celebrants like the swarming flies that marked some rotting carcass in lowland marshes of his home. As he watched, one stood and walked carefully back across the sand to disappear through a small gate. He bore a stone vial in both hands, cradling it like an infant.

Behind them, the court chattered convivially. Servants produced skins of agave wine, which delighted those in attendance. Yax Yapaat, as usual, ignored the rising song of voices behind him. Nothing stirred the King's icy and imperturbable mien. He bowed to Cayucali. The more attentive members of the court had the presence of mind to mimic his bow. Yax Yapaat took no notice of either those who did, or those who did not. His bright green eyes filled themselves with the image of the kneeling warrior.

"You have no interest in honoring me," Yax Yapaat said. "I understand. You are not here of your own will." He drew his cloak around his gaunt shoulders, though the sun shone and the day was warm. "In a way, you are right to deny me obeisance."

"I am glad you think so," Cayucali said. "Come closer; I will deny you a great deal of obeisance."

Yax Yapaat lifted a hand to forestall the punishing blow from the men of the guard.

"We are the planets themselves," Yax Yapaat said. "Do you understand? We move along our orbits, we fulfill our purposes. Your purpose is only aided by the black hate I see in your eyes. The fulfillment of your purpose will come sooner or later—after today, I think later. You are a warrior worthy of admiration. I hope for your continued success in the liturgy. Not for my sake, I who am withered and empty, I who have little time left. But for Kalak Mool's. For Tezca's."

Then Yax Yapaat turned away, and Tezca was left to stare at Cayucali, who held his gaze. He made a sour face, then smoothed it away. Tezca turned to follow Yax Yapaat.

"Tezca," Cayucali said. "Wait. Listen."

Tezca turned back, his lips twisting into an unconscious sneer. "What do you have to say to me? I have had enough from you to last a lifetime. I care not what the King says, I hope they take *your* blood from this sand."

Deadly anger flashed across the warrior's face. Something in Tezca flinched; he took a step backward before he mastered himself.

He forced himself to continue. "Will you apologize for

breaking my arms? Will you apologize for shaming me before the Prince of Tolcalax? Will you admit now that--"

"No," Cayucali said. "I will not."

Tezca flushed. "Then we have nothing to speak about."

"We are countrymen, despite everything," Cayucali said. "We came over the pass together, fled the ruins together. You can trust none here but me."

"I would trust every man and woman here before I trusted you, old fool."

Cayucali bit back his reply. Tezca glanced over his shoulder. Yax Yapaat conversed with a man who wore scarlet macaw feathers in his hair and bore a blade of blackglass at his belt. The white-clad priests completed their grisly tasks in the sand and vanished into the depths of the arena. The wind tugged small drifts of sand against the edges of his feet. The chatter of the court began to shift toward the evening's entertainment.

"Something is wrong," he said. "It makes no sense! The cursed priest is keeping something from you."

"Of course you would think so," Tezca said. "You are a prisoner. Perhaps if you win the liturgy, you will earn your freedom. Then you can return to Batun, and die there."

Across the arena, Commander Oahqui waved. He shouted for Cayucali to return through the arena gate. Tezca turned and began to trudge after the royal procession.

"Can you go home?" Cayucali asked, his voice imploring. "You are a prisoner too."

Tezca turn back, and smiled. "Why would I want to go home?"

Dark Healing

Gentle footsteps crossed the bare stone floor behind Cayucali. In his dream, they were the sound of polished black stones falling into a stream. Their mounded humps made a curving path through the slow-moving water. He crossed the stream. Midway across, it dissolved around him, and he stared at a square-vaulted ceiling carved with vines and twining serpents.

"I have been here before," Cayucali said. He tried to sit up, but his head spun. "And I could not stand then, either."

"If you stand, you will tear your stitches," a kind voice said. "You must not waste my efforts like that."

Then a familiar face appeared at his side. Xhoc smiled down at him and placed a cool hand on his shoulder. The kindness in her expression was unfeigned, though it seemed to mask some deeper preoccupation. He shifted his shoulders until he found a position that did not ache or sting. The tips of his fingers pushed against the long gash on his belly he had received in the arena.

"I thank you for your efforts," Cayucali said. "Your sutures are excellent."

"You are courteous," Xhoc said. "Appreciative patients are so rare. It is good to hear."

Cayucali craned his neck back to see her better. Upside down, her expression was difficult to read. Her large eyes studied him. She seemed to hesitate.

"Warrior—"

"Cayucali."

"Who are you?" She put a hand in front of her mouth to hide an embarrassed smile. "I only mean—you are courteous, when you speak at all. And though your dialect is not my own, you speak as an educated man. You are no common slave."

"What use to distinguish among slaves?" Cayucali asked. "Whatever I might have been, I am to be consumed and digested for the sport of gaping fishes, just the same as those I butchered today. They were my countrymen, you know."

"I am sorry," Xhoc said.

"Not so sorry," he said bitterly. "You heal me that I might be further expended on the sand of your wicked arena. You stitch my wounds but keep me docile with cunning powders and tinctures. If you healed me too well, I would cease to be good sport."

Xhoc's face fell, her eyes now sorrowful. "I am sorry for that too," she whispered.

Cayucali stretched out his arm, though it protested the use with pain like burning spiders crawling. He touched her arm. She wiped her eyes with the palm of her hand.

"Please," he said. "Ignore me. That was not courteous."

"No," she said. "You see clearly. You speak truly. Yet I have no choice but to fulfill my role, while it is mine to fulfill. It is the same for you."

"I have heard it said that we are planets, we follow our orbits."

"You spoke to my father," Xhoc said.

"He spoke to me."

"In truth, Itzamma is the astrologer, not my father. My father is like you. A great warrior, a great prince. Or so I remember him, when I was young."

"You are young still," Cayucali said. "And it has been a long time since I was much of a warrior, and longer still since I was anything like a prince."

"Again, you are courteous," Xhoc said. "I wish you were a guest of lower honor here, so that we could walk in the gardens. Tezca says that Batun has magnificent gardens, with strange flowers from the distant north. Is it true that Batun trades with the men from that land?"

"Tezca knows better than I," he said. "It has been many years since I was in Batun. I am an exile. He is in the favor of the King there, to my great sorrow."

She arched an eyebrow, then smiled. "You have a pattern of getting yourself into trouble. Yet I am not sure Tezca is as favored as you think. Why else would he remain willingly remain here? I have spent some little time with him—

"Now I must apologize to you, for bringing him here to plague you," Cayucali said.

Xhoc laughed. "He is only a young man. He has nothing to his name yet. So he pretends. You are a great man, with a great name, though I do not know it. Do not protest, anyone with eyes would mark you as a man of breeding and renown. Tezca could learn and make his own name, with time and opportunity. But Kalak Mool is an old city with many secrets. I fear neither of you have much time."

"I learn slowly, if at all," he said. "But if I get myself out of trouble here, maybe I can get myself out of trouble in Batun too. Perhaps Tezca will tire of his spiteful games and yearn for home. And you cannot give me my freedom, but I can win it in the liturgy."

At that, she turned away from him. Her dark hair curtained her face. She collected herself quickly and gave him a wan smile.

"Have you not heard? The liturgy is made to discover the worthiest sacrifice. The victor's blood is prized above all others. His skin is a powerful relic; his hands a great trophy. You will win freedom of a sort. Your body will be eaten to strengthen our warriors. The glory of your soul will draw the Turquoise Serpent through the veil and into the vessel. You are the key to Tezca's coronation."

Cayucali let his arm fall. It hung limply over the side of the stone bier. He stared at the carved ceiling for a time. His mind returned to the white field of the arena. Some of what Yax Yapaat said now held a new and bleaker meaning. He was more right than he knew, though there was no pleasure in it. He tried to warn Tezca of danger—he should have warned himself. Victory would not save his life.

"So," he said, "I am Tezca's ladder to the Waterlily Throne."

"You or another," Xhoc said.

He closed his eyes, suddenly exhausted. He cursed the wizard, not for being a wizard, but for being Tezca. Stubborn, immature Tezca. It was almost like having a child. He laughed bitterly at that. Xhoc's hand was cool on his brow. Her sweet, sad voice murmured in his ear, coaxing him into sleep.

Revulsion

❦

Tezca wrapped his thickest cloak around himself. The colonnaded terrace outside his suite was vulnerable to the night wind, and the night wind was frigid. A few smears of reddish torchlight marred the darkness, but overhead the stars were bright. The moon was a bone fishhook just above the horizon. Tezca paced restlessly.

Then he straightened. He stalked off the terrace and through his suite, emerging into the cool night. He fluttered like a moth up stone stairways and along colonnades. He encountered no one. The common people of Kalak Mool had begun to gather in the lower city for the King's procession, later in the night, and the grounds of the palace complex were not patrolled.

Still, he breathed in relief when he came to the archway that led to Itzamma's garden. He let his cloak fall around him as he reached out to push the wooden door. It swung silently open. He passed through the wall from the city into the garden. When the door closed, it was as though the entire citadel vanished. There was only the garden; the densely planted trees heavy with parasitical climbers and flowers and crawling with small life, the flowering asters and the vines that crept along across narrow gravel paths.

He followed the path past the little fountain and the tile where his sigil fractured the earth. He glimpsed the walls of the garden from time to time. They peeked out from beyond the march of trees, from behind the net of green vines. But they were always distant. No matter what path he took, he never seemed in danger of approaching the edge of the garden. The scent of aster was strong.

The path brought him at last to the wooden palace miniature. As if mired in some waking dream, he opened the shrewcote and clasped three of the huddling little animals to his breast. He carried them to the stone table. There on the table was a blade of knapped volcanic glass, as black and silky as the night sky. Taking that razor edge in his hand, he made careful cuts across the throat and other surface arteries of each shrew. He coated his hands in their blood and reshaped the life of the shrews into something else.

An image appeared before his eyes; a mature man in a long belted tunic. He too stood in a garden. As Tezca watched, he plucked the dry and wilted heads of dahlias, casting them into the garden beds. Though the image was murky, the scene was familiar. He focused and the details sharpened. The man worked for another minute. The set of his shoulders, relaxed at first, seemed to tighten as Tezca watched. At some point, Tezca knew it was Master Tall Deer he watched.

Then Tall Deer turned. His face was impassive, but Tezca heard the surprise in his voice. He wiped his hands and arrayed them at his waist in a gesture of repose.

"I gather this is no dream or vision," Tall Deer said. "You appear to me as an image of yourself, faint and ghostly. Have you traveled through some ethereal pathway? Are you here in truth?"

"A vision of you appears to me also," Tezca said. "Pruning flowers in your garden in Batun."

Tall Deer nodded. "I am doing so in waking life. Tell me Tezca, if Tezca you truly are—what were you studying before you left Batun?"

Tezca flushed. "The progression of circular forms across the tail of the iguana. I failed your examination."

"Yes," Tall Deer nodded. "You did. You have not returned to Batun," he observed.

"I was waylaid," Tezca said.

"When shall I expect you in the capital?" he asked.

"My hosts have been generous. When I can leave them without insult, I will return. I am cognizant of my duties and lessons."

Tall-Deer smirked. "Your absence is keenly felt, but I shall endure." He resumed plucking the dead flowerheads. "Will you return in time for the Feast of the Jaguar?"

"I hope to."

"Do not fret if you cannot," Tall-Deer said. "Uctli will take your place. He has become a great favorite of the court, you know. He sits on the council with your father often. The King has spoken well of him."

Tezca kept his face impassive. "My family's success honors me."

"As your success would honor your family," Tall Deer said. "But as you have not returned yet, I do not know what to think about your appointment in Tolcalax. I have had troubling reports from the Prince. We must discuss these."

"We shall," Tezca said.

Tall Deer stood, groaning as he straightened his spine. He was in his garden; the stone archway to his courtyard framed him. "How have you accomplished this vision? Have you finally mastered the fourth iteration of radial symmetry?"

Tezca paled. Why had he not expected the question? He

tried to sever the connection, to let the threads of the vision dissolve, to return to the garden. But Tall Deer frowned.

"The vision fades," he said. "You have not mastered the fourth iteration after all." Then his eyes widened. "But this is not radial symmetry. This is not sigilry at all. Tezca, where are you? What have you done? Who taught you this? Done you understand the danger you are in at this very moment?"

Tezca said nothing.

"The pass over the mountain,," Tall-Deer mused. "You are in Kalak Mool. Do you understand the forces you are toying with? Do you have any comprehension of the heresy you now commit? Return to Batun immediately. You must atone for this. The council will determine a suitable punishment for you."

"But I have only sought to learn! I have the respect of the King, of the High Priest—I will be a great asset to the King!"

"You have their respect—ha!"Tall-Deer snapped, his voice cold and imperious. "The Serpent Kings are perfidious, rotten at their core. Their accursed deity drives them to endless depravity. You are nothing but a foolish boy. Cease your prattling and return to me at once. Your father and King Chimal will hear of this."

Tall Deer dispersed the threads of the vision with a perfunctory gesture of dismissal, and the image unraveled. The scent of aster flowers filled the air of the garden. The stars were a spray of jewels on a velvet cloth.

Parade

Wild music surged in the broad and crowded avenue. Players blew gourd-carved horns and whistles shaped from conch-shells. They plucked stringed instruments and pounded massive drums of stretched hide. There was no order to the music that accompanied the procession making its way through the citadel of Kalak Mool. The spontaneous amalgamation of each little band's melodies and rhythms contributed to the shifting, evolving whole, like a kaleidescope of sound that followed them down throught the citadel.

The procession was part of the liturgy, and Cayucali was accorded a place of honor in the van, though his wrists were once again bound. With him were the remaining celebrants, led by Zolin. Pactli sat beside him in a wagon drawn by great rams with ancient curling horns. A rush burned behind the driver and bathed them in a wavering light. Pactli was transformed. The normally taciturn warrior smiled and waved at the people who thronged the avenue. He even rested his hand on Cayucali's shoulder.

"Is it not fine to be loved by the people?" he asked.

"It is," Cayucali said. "While it lasts."

"For one of us, it shall last forever," Pactli said. "Zolin was right about you, warrior. I should not have doubted him. You honor the liturgy. You honor the Serpent."

"You know what will happen if you win?"

Pactli looked at him as though he were mad. "Know? Of course I know. I would not have volunteered otherwise."

At the head of the procession, Yax Yapaat and Itzamma spoke intimately, ignoring the tumult of the raucous crowd. Tezca rode beside them, waving and smiling. Oahqui, leading a marching column of Blue Knives beside them, offered grave nods to the gathered and adoring people. Zolin rode behind the column of celebrants. Before the procession began, he had slipped Cayucali several long cigars enfolded by a tobacco leaf.

Cayucali unwrapped the leaf now and offered one to Pactli, who grinned wider still. Cayucali leaned forward and lit his cigar from the burning rush, then lit Pactli's from his own.

"I know the victor will be you or I," Pactli said. "And now I know that whoever is victorious, the Serpent will receive a worthy sacrifice."

"Stop," Cayucali said. "I cannot talk about sacrifices any more. You are giving me a headache."

Something boomed ahead of them, setting his ears ringing, and a burst of scintillating flame filled the evening sky. A rainbow of shifting colors painted the procession in jade, lazuli, and amethyst. The already disorderly procession collapsed into greater disarray.

The rams that drew his wagon screamed and reared and bolted from their position in the parade. Pactli was pitched from the wagon as it careened against the corner of a house. He tumbled through the air, his look of amused shock illuminated in the ember glow of the cigar clamped between his teeth.

Cayucali clutched the rail of the wagon desperately as the

rams fled down a narrow alley into the dark and winding labyrinth of the citadel. The wagon's crude wooden wheels clattered on the rough cobbles and the sound was like echoing thunder in the narrow alleyway. One tremendous bounce sent his own cigar spinning away. He nearly followed it when he released the rail to try to catch it.

After a harrowing ride deep into the citadel, the rams forgot the terror of the burst of rainbow flame and slowed to a trot, then halted. Cayucali climbed out of the wagon and lit his last cigar on the still-burning rush. He found himself in a small plaza with a low fountain. He paced the plaza, his heart racing from the wagon's ferocious course, laughter bubbling from his belly. He was having fun—he almost failed to recognize the emotion

He laughed truly then. He was alone for the first time since he violated the King's edict and cracked Tezca's arms in Tolcalax. Alone for the first time since he violated his exile. He could hardly hear the clamor of the procession, far away and high above him on the citadel. He had the quaint plaza to himself.

He plunged his hands into the fountain and splashed his face with the cool water. He put his back to the wall of the fountain and leaned his neck back against the rim while he debated whether to take the opportunity to escape that had fallen into his lap.

The problem, as always, was Tezca. The idiot wizard was enamored of the masters of this accursed kingdom; some black glamour deceived him. If Batun had forgotten the lessons of the Morning War, perhaps it deserved what Tezca would bring it.

Cayucali shook his head and blew out a cloud of smoke. Perhaps he was a sentimental old fool, but old loyalties bound him tight. Whatever fate Chimal had in mind for him, he would face on his own terms. He owed Chimal that much and more. And if he rescued a favored son of Batun and disrupted the coronation of a Serpent King before Chimal issued his judgment, so much the better.

Justice in Batun was harsh, but fair. Great deeds and true loyalty were always rewarded. If Cayucali snatched a prize away from the Serpent Kingdom and saved the son of one of Chimal's Councilors by doing so, Chimal would be forced to be lenient. Of course, all that depended on Tezca testifying on his behalf.

He was still alone with his musings in the plaza. Before him was a carpenter's shop, empty and dark beneath an awning of dried and woven reeds. Wreathed in fragrant smoke, Cayucali pushed aside the swinging gate to the shop and wandered through the orderly racks of tools. He eyed the saws and augurs and admired the half-finished carvings that rested on the hardwood workbenches. He lifted a rough bone file from the bench and tucked it through his belt, inside his tunic.

A soft footstep sounded behind him.

"There you are," someone said.

Cayucali spun, his shoulders tensed. Zolin watched him from the entrance to the carpenter's shop. How long had he watched?

"No need for that," Zolin said with a smile. He held up his hand in a gesture of peace. "They have the procession under control, mostly. Couple of stray wagons to round up. Something the little wizard boy did, I heard. Come back with me. I will drive the rams."

"I could have been a long way away," Cayucali said.

"Maybe," Zolin said. "But you are still here. So come back with me. If you flee, they will find you. They will whip me, if I am lucky. Take wisdom from an old man. Do not fight too hard. Live a little longer."

Cayucali left the carpentry shop and returned to the procession, and the wild music.

Picnic

The day after the procession dawned red and overcast, promising rain. Tezca met the dawn with a haggard stare and rubbed his sleepless eyes. The vision of Tall Deer and the royal procession through the citadel the night before left him with much to ponder. He sat among the stumps of waxen candles, burned to their roots like the remains of some saw-felled glade. A persistent wind came in through the terrace, wet and cool.

Some minutes later, he passed along the covered paths and winding stairs of the citadel to seek out Itzamma in the garden. The sun was a hazy white disk behind thickening clouds. Lonely raindrops stained the old stone. He kept his hood up against the rain and against searching eyes, but he passed no one.

He came upon Itzamma kneeling in the garden. The priest greeted him with a quick smile, then cast a distracted look toward the grey skies above.

"Not a good day to garden," Itzamma said. "Not really a good day for anything." He seemed to come to some inner conclusion. "Except perhaps to visit the King's Isle. The procession last night put me in the mood for diversion."

He stood and stretched, swinging his hips and pulling his arms across his chest, then made for the entrance. "Come along. We must ready the boatman."

Tezca and Itzamma came to a wide and warm lagoon connected to the royal complex, fed by a secret spring. Its surface was choked with lily pads and hyacinths and shaded by tall canopies of woven reeds

The boatman was readied. He poled his flat barque across the surface of the lagoon. Its prow divided the green mat of water plants and sent clouds of dragonflies buzzing into the air. They passed through a channel and the water rippled away from them, making quiet lapping sounds against the stone.

The channel opened and the barque floated into an expanse of clearer, bluer water pierced in the center by an island that thrust from the bed of the lagoon. It was capped by a graceful and well-proportioned palace surrounded by sprays of flowers and carefully tended orchards. The slate of dark clouds left its colors muted and greyed.

The barque coasted to a stop and they climbed out at the quay. The short quay led to a covered walkway, through the gardens and toward the palace. The ferryman tied the barque to the quay and made a deep bow toward them before tipping his broad-brimmed hat over his eyes and reclining beneath the canopy that covered the rear of the barque. The rain fell harder, but they were dry beneath the covered walk.

"I saw something strange in the garden today," Itzamma said. "A drop or two of blood on the workbench. And the shrews seemed startled."

Tezca glanced across the walkway. A gentle smile tugged at the priest's thin mouth.

"I tried what you showed me," Tezca said. "Last night, before the procession."

Itzamma nodded. "I thought perhaps a hawk, but the

doors of the shrewcote were closed. You left me a fine puzzle."

The covered path led to the entry of the palace. Itzamma produced a delicate key and pushed the heavy door open. The palace was dark and empty. Itzamma moved along the walls, lifting the covers from the open windows and bringing light and air into the room.

Tezca gasped. In the great parlor of the palace, lining the thick stone walls, wooden shelves strained under the weight of books, scrolls, and carved tablets. It was a library.

As Tezca craned his neck to stare at the room, Itzamma finished opening the windows. He limped toward the great stone hearth in the center of the far wall and knelt to kindle a fire. He spun the hand drill briskly and soon had a tiny ember smoking. He fed it straw, then splinters, and in a few minutes had a modest flame amid the white ash.

"I could have started the fire with a sigil," Tezca said.

Itzamma shrugged. "I like to kindle by hand. It is easier, in the long run. And safer. Magic always carries danger—especially the bloody kind."

He arranged a few larger split logs in the hearth to warm near the flame, then dusted the ash from his hands. He vanished through a small doorway then returned a moment later bearing a clay bottle and a great slab of rolled, cured meat. These he placed on an elegant table beside a padded seat and, retrieving a particular book, settled into the seat and into the silence.

Tezca found a book of his own. He unfolded it to find it painted with the story of two gods, brothers hunted by some pale beast that dwelt in caverns deep beneath the earth. He did not recognize the story. He took the seat opposite Itzamma, who offered him liquor from the clay bottle. The fire, now dancing over a bed of glowing coals, radiated warmth. The sound of the rain outside and the waves of heat from the hearth brought him to the edge of sleep.

"Did it work?" Itzamma asked, his own eyes now closed.

The question brought Tezca back to waking, though it took him some moments before he recalled the shrews in the garden.

"It worked," he said. "I spoke to Tall Deer, my master in Batun."

"Impressive," Itzamma said. He lifted his eyebrows without opening his eyes. "But then, we must expect great things from the vessel. What did Tall Deer say?"

"He was furious. I am to attend him in Batun immediately, for judgment."

There was a pause. The fire burned. The rain fell.

"Will you?" Itzamma asked.

Tezca stared into the fire drowsily.

"That fool has no right to pronounce judgment on me. I would rather be King in Kalak Mool than a whipped dog in Batun."

"I was sure you would make the right decision," Itzamma said. "Yet I am still glad to hear it. You will never be a whipped dog, there or here. With you as King of Kalak Mool, we will rebuild the Serpent's armies and fill his coffers with tribute. We will reignite the fires of war and rediscover great sorceries to devastate our enemies."

Tezca nodded, though he seemed not to hear. "Thank you, Itzamma," he said.

"For what?"

He waved his hands around. "For a pleasant day in a fine library. For teaching me. For everything."

"You are most welcome, Your Highness."

Tezca slipped into sleep. Itzamma's dark eyes glittered with reflected fire.

Glory

⁂

Cayucali slid in and out of sleep. Though the dormitory was quiet and dark, he was unable to find comfort in the small bunk. A dream vision plagued him. It arrested his attention and he could think or dream of nothing else. In it, a woman whose beauty was incomparable, sidereal, stood before him. She was unfamiliar to him, yet he loved her immediately. Her face was fixed in revulsion.

To see disgust on her beautiful face pierced his heart; that it was directed toward him was too much to bear. He felt some small relief when he turned to see that it was not he at whom she stared with such disgust, but instead at some shadowy thing that curled and slithered behind him, in the darkness among the stars.

Then he started awake, Zolin's hand on his shoulder.

"Last one," Zolin said. "Are you ready?"

"Last what?" Cayucali swung his neck from side to side. Vertebrae cracked. He slid out of the low bunk and shook out the night's aches. Zolin was already moving toward the archway that led from the dormitory. The beds around him were empty.

"Last celebration," he said. "Last fight. Win today, become the champion of the Liturgy of Coalescence."

"An honor I could do without," Cayucali said. "I would rather keep wearing my skin."

"Then die in the sand," Zolin said with a grin. "But first, eat. Then pray. I will find you when it is time."

Cayucali ignored Zolin's orders. He was not hungry. He did not like to eat until the danger passed. He did not know what nightmarish battle awaited him. A bellyful of grain porridge would only make him slow and stupid.

He neglected too the shrine to Kalak Mool's multitudinous deities. The hideous serpent in the center of the shrine glowered at him as he passed. The scales of its belly glowed dull red in the coal light that flooded from the braziers surrounding the effigy. Reptilian eyes regarded him with contempt, and perhaps a certain hunger.

He spent his remaining time in the room with the mats, loosening his limbs and enjoying the stillness of morning.

"Are you ready?" Zolin asked again, appearing in the archway. In his hand, he bore Cayucali's ironwood blade.

"I am never ready." Cayucali grinned, taking the sword. "But this makes me feel better."

"Come along," Zolin said. "The arena is prepared. The crowd has gathered. The King awaits."

Cayucali followed Zolin along the familiar path that led to the long tunnel, the thornwood gate, the white sand of the arena.

"I smoked the cigars you gave me," Cayucali said.

"Good," Zolin said. "Don't delay your pleasures."

"What will you do after the liturgy?" Cayucali asked.

"There will be other seasons, other festivals. The Paddock will be filled again. I will tell the celebrants to go here, go there, and see that the cooks have meals ready. I will give them cigars, and curse the work that falls to me."

They walked side by side down the long tunnel and

stopped before the arena gate. Squares of sunlight patterned the stone floor. White sand ebbed across the stone like foam on the beach.

"A pleasure, Zolin," Cayucali said.

"Likewise," Zolin said.

Then he dragged the gate aside, and Cayucali stepped into the gleaming sand of the arena. A lone figure emerged from the far side of the arena, a dark blur in the blazing sunshine. Cayucali approached the center of the arena, holding his blade loosely at his side. He came face to face with Pactli, who bore a blade edged with black glass.

"Did I not say it would be one of us?" Pactli asked. He bowed.

"I would rather it were neither of us," Cayucali said.

Pactli hefted his blade. "You are still reluctant. I am sorry. But I beg you, do not fail to give your utmost." He took a cautious step forward, then another, holding his blade before him in a position of guard.

Cayucali lifted his own sword. The corded leather that bound the hilt felt good in his palm. He was tired of choosing between two hateful options. The hardened point of his sword flicked through the air. Pactli paused to let it go by, then continued his advance. Pactli moved methodically, relentlessly, pressuring Cayucali, ignoring his feints, deflecting his searching attacks. He presented a plodding, implacable defense.

Cayucali decided to try something different. He swung his blade again, extending himself a bit further. Pactli let it whistle past, nodding to himself at the miniscule error.

The momentum of the heavy blade tugged Cayucali forward, and his foot stuttered forward to regain his balance. Pactli struck in an instant, erupting from behind his cautious shell like a crocodile from beneath dark waters. His wide shoulders bunched, and his blade turned in the air and hurtled toward Cayucali's forward leg.

Cayucali's smile was fierce. He drew the exposed leg back, allowing the blackglass blade to swing harmless through empty air. Overbalanced without the support of his leg, Cayucali fell forward. He brought his sword over his shoulder like a hammer, the cords of his forearms taut as ropes. The ironwood blade screamed through the air like an eagle diving.

Pactli's eyes widened. Then the flat of the blade struck him in the forehead. His skull rang like a hammerstroke on an anvil and his legs buckled beneath him. He fell to his back, his arms sprawling apart in the white sand. His hand opened. His sword rolled from his fingers. Cayucali held the point of his sword over Pactli's chest, his own great chest heaving like a bellows. The roar of the crowd was deafening.

Beneath his blade, Pactli stirred. He came to his senses quickly. His eyes focused on the point of the blade, then on Cayucali above. He smiled, nodded.

Cayucali lifted his blade, then let it rest on his shoulder. He took a few steps away from Pactli and sat down in the sand, and did not move.

The sound of crowd faltered, then redoubled, audibly furious. Pactli climbed to his knees. A thick red welt was rising between his eyes. He bowed his head to Cayucali.

Then he drew a small blackglass knife from beneath his tunic. He punched the sliver blade into his throat and dragged it through the soft tissues there. Bright blood fountained into the white sand. Pactli collapsed forward. His blood pooled around him, tendrils of it stretching toward where Cayucali sat still.

White-robed priests rushed into the arena and knelt around the fallen warrior, collecting his blood from the sodden sand.

Cayucali's heart grew hard.

The Audience

Tezca was drunk.

The sumptuous colors and rich scents of the feast made a sensational tapestry on the pavilion atop the Temple of the Serpent. Away, tucked under some secondary pavilion or hidden in some secret niche, musicians plucked at strings and pounded drumskins, filling the world with a fiery, pulsating song.

The long, low tables were again piled with the king's bounty. Tall braziers sent clouds of aromatic smoke to diffuse beneath the pavilion. A round, red sun hung like a ruby between the peaks of mountains on the western side of the vale.

Tezca sat at the King's own table and hated every moment of it. He crumbled a maize cake between his fingers, taking idle bites between sipping at his cup. Itzamma sat beside him, absorbed in conversation with his neighbor concerning the growing of gourds according to the phases of the moon. The conversation was academic, and therefore dull, though the man held a grim reputation as the potentate of one of Kalak Mool's outlying settlements.

On Tezca's other side, Yax Yapaat, the Serpent King, sat

overlooking the feast on a raised seat that separated him from Tezca, and from Xhoc on his far side. His polished jade eyes betrayed no fraction of interest in the revelry. The thin line of his mouth was sealed as tightly as a tomb.

Xhoc, on the other hand, was lively and animated. She laughed and smiled, conversing freely and enthusiastically. But not with him. He glanced at the floor and smirked. By chance, the sigil he'd scratched into the stone at his first audience with Yax Yapaat was still there. He deepened it idly with a knife as he stared at Xhoc.

He scowled. With him, she was morose and nearly silent on the subject of his ascension. It was the giant exile Cayucali who captured her attention and held it with an easy warmth. The entire feast was in his honor; he, the Champion of Kalak Mool, the victor of the Liturgy of Coalescence.

It comforted him only a little that the feast was a sort of fattening of the capybara before the slaughter. That fact did not seem to concern Cayucali. He ate, drank, and spoke with unfeigned pleasure. Tezca lifted his own cup again, as Cayucali explained the finer points of cooking a capybara in a pit buried in the earth. Sweet flower wine filled Tezca's mouth. He wished he could feel so free when speaking to Xhoc.

As the court ate its fill, lords and ladies began to move about the pavilion. They formed small circles, laughing and eating toothsome delicacies; cocoa sweetened with honey and spiced with smoked peppers, candied yucca flowers, and warm fried plantain.

A steady stream of Kalak Mool's highest nobility passed him by in order to make their obeisances to Cayucali. Cayucali, for his part, received these with a grace worthy of any king's court, though it was perhaps only in the haze of the flower wine that Tezca could admit that to himself.

Yet should they not have paid *him* their respects as well, and in greater measure? He would soon be their king. If Yax

Yapaat gave them a loose leash and a soft hand, he would not be so generous.

He left his seat at the King's table and wandered around the edge of the pavilion, pausing near the tall braziers for warmth until the fragrant smoke became cloying. Though he had been in Kalak Mool for some weeks now, he knew few of the gathered nobility. Most of his time was spent cloistered with Itzamma, practicing the subtleties of blood and performing exercises Itzamma promised would prepare him to commune with the Turquoise Serpent.

But Itzamma was not interested in conversation tonight—at least, not with him. Tezca allowed a servant to pour him another cup of flower wine. He lifted the cup and had nearly drained it when something eclipsed the light of the tall brazier and drenched him in shadow.

"Have you grown tired of the princess?" Tezca asked.

"Xhoc?" Cayucali said. "It is you I want to speak with."

"We have trodden this ground," Tezca said. "What have you to say to me?"

Cayucali crossed his arms. "You are drunk."

"And?" Tezca tipped the cup again and the last of the flower wine coated his throat. He looked around for the servant with the ewer.

Cayucali laughed.

Tezca flushed and turned to walk away, but the giant's thick hand caught him by the shoulder and spun him back around.

"That is fair," Cayucali said, still chuckling. He waved his hand at a passing servant, who filled both their cups. "Maybe I should follow you."

"What do you want?" Tezca said.

"To apologize," Cayucali said. "For breaking your arms. I am sorry."

Tezca searched for something to say. He failed, and so he said nothing.

"They plan to kill me," Cayucali said. "A sacrifice to their disgusting snake god. The entire purpose of the Liturgy of Coalescence was to find the strongest sacrifice for the ritual of the coronation. I will not be here for that."

Tezca was still nonplussed by Cayucali's apology. "I—Why—?" he stammered.

Cayucali's brow wrinkled, then lifted. "That does not surprise you. You already knew. I see."

"Well, Itzamma—"

"You have agreed to succeed Yax Yapaat as King of Kalak Mool," Cayucali said. "Do not deny it."

"I do not!" Tezca snapped. "I will become King, and be treated like a man instead of a feral beast. What of it?"

Cayucali shook his head. "What of it? Must I die for your arrogance? Why should I not simply kill you now? I could do so and be gone from this accursed city tonight."

"Then do it," Tezca said, his voice hot, his words slurred. "Begone, if you think you can. The Blue Knives will find you. We all move in our orbits, like the planets."

"Not me," Cayucali said. "And you do not have to either. Look at Yax Yapaat! He is a husk of a man, a shadow of what he was. There is nothing of Yax Yapaat left—there is only the fragment of the Serpent festering and seething within him. So will it be with you. You will be consumed day by day until only the Serpent remains. Then, when there is nothing left to feed on, they will hold another Liturgy of Coalescence!"

Tezca hurled his cup at the ground and clenched his fists. He leaned forward and bit off every word with fervor he did not know he possessed.

"In three days, I will drink your blood and become King of Kalak Mool. King—do you understand? King! There will not be another Coalescence if I do not permit it. And I will not!"

"I will not harm you, Tezca. I am sorry for harming you before. I saw you as only a wizard, and not a man. That has changed. We are countrymen, and I will not leave here without you. I beg you—consider my warning. You are not the true power in this land."

"Leave or stay, what is that to me?" Tezca shouted. "I will be King!" Then he stumbled through the crowd gathered for the feast and away into the darkened pathways of the citadel while the moon soared high overhead.

Discovery

❦

Tezca followed Itzamma up an endless chain of stairways until it seemed they would climb above the quickly setting sun. Spindly clouds marched across the sky like sand dunes and reflected the red sun. The wind grew wilder with every step into the bloody sky until Tezca wanted to put his hands to the stairs to steady himself. Itzamma climbed fearlessly. Tezca pulled his hood up and followed.

His lungs burned in the crisp air, his legs ached with every step. Above him, the citadel merged into the slope of the mountain itself. Itzamma led him to a place he called the pinnacle, the highest place in Kalak Mool, there to receive a private audience with Yax Yapaat on the eve of his coronation.

At first, Tezca was excited. He had questions for Yax Yapaat, questions concerning the rulership of the kingdom—its methods, its people, its resources. He needed to understand Kalak Mool better to rule it well.

It was even fitting that he undertake the arduous pilgrimage to the pinnacle in order to speak with the King. Or so he thought while still at the bottom of this endless stair. Now, he wondered whether he would blown off the face of the mountain, or tumble down after his heart burst in his chest.

"Are we close?" He called to Itzamma.

The priest paused, glanced down at Tezca, then pointed. Tezca followed the gesture. At first, he saw nothing but bare stone, orange lichen, and flowering gorse. Then he saw the tower, very near to where they now stood.

It stood in a wrinkle of the mountain and seemed to wear the mountain's own skin; its stone surfaces were unworked and covered in the same lichens. Gorse and sandwort sprouted from the seams in its stone. Even now, resuming the climb, the tower appeared to vanish into the mountain.

After a few more turns, the stair led to a small arched doorway. Itzamma produced a key and pushed the door open, motioning for Tezca to enter. Rushlights lit the small room, but there was little to see. Only another stairwell, spiraling through the ceiling to the top of the tower.

Tezca scowled, but mounted these stairs too, until he came to their end and found himself in a simple, bare room. Coals in a stone brazier warmed the space, but a cold wind blew in from the arched doorway to the balcony. Outside, the King waited.

Itzamma nodded toward the doorway, then took a seat near the brazier. Tezca strode onto the balcony and gasped. From the pinnacle, he could see the entirety of Kalak Mool unfurled like a sail. Yax Yapaat leaned against the rail of the balcony, staring out into the vale like a hawk watching prey. Finally, he turned to Tezca.

"You will be King soon," Yax Yapaat said. His face was pale and gaunt, his voice frigid. He seemed like one of the dead, except for a mad flame in his eyes.

"I will be honored to lead Kalak Mool," Tezca said. "But I have—"

"You will not lead Kalak Mool," Yax Yapaat said. "The Turquoise Serpent leads Kalak Mool. Always."

"Of course," Tezca said. "But I am not ready."

"Itzamma says you are ready. The liturgy is nearly complete. That is all that is required. When you came to us, I told you I would pray that you would be able to bear the preparation."

"It has been difficult," Tezca said. "But I have done so."

"Nearly so," Yax Yapaat said. "You understand the necessity of the sacrifice?"

"The power derived from the sacrifice is what parts the veil, that the Serpent may move freely in this world."

"You will accept the sacrifice of your countryman?" Yax Yapaat asked. "You will wear his skin, take his blood?"

"I will," Tezca said.

Yax Yapaat nodded. "Good. Then all that is left is for the Serpent to be released from my own form."

"How does that happen?"

"The same way, of course. A sharp blade drawn across the throat."

Tezca studied the land beneath him. Cayucali's warning echoed in his head, but he pushed it aside. What did he care if Yax Yapaat wanted to die? So much the better for him. Something moving in the distance caught his eye, something dark passing across the clouds.

"If that is your will," Tezca said. "I accept it."

"Good," the King said. "Then return to your rooms and prepare yourself. The ritual will begin tonight, when the planets are in agreement. Itzamma will guide you through what is necessary."

Yax Yapaat waved his hand and returned his attention to the valley below. His face was as still and impassive as the mountain itself. He betrayed no hint of sorrow or fear. He spoke of his own impending death with terrifying calm. His steadfast disinterest cast a spell on Tezca.

When Yax Yapaat said nothing more, Tezca left the balcony for the warmth of the tower.

"Was that all?" Itzamma asked.

"He said you will tell me everything else I need to know," Tezca said.

"And so I shall." Itzamma stood. "Though my duties force me to leave even the paltry warmth this brazier provides, I am ever my master's servant. Come along and ask your questions while we walk. I am sure you have many."

They made the long journey down into thicker air, into the living parts of the colossal citadel, and spoke as they did. The red sun slipped lower and the spindle clouds stretched away into an infinite purple sky. Bright stars burned holes in the cloud cover and lit their way into the royal palace. Finally, Tezca asked the question that clawed at his ribs.

"Why does Yax Yapaat consign himself to death?"

"It is as it must be," Itzamma said. "He and his household have lived as the vessel of Xicuoatl. For Xicuoatl to imbue a new vessel, the old must undergo the final sacrifice, lest any part of the Xicuoatl be retained, and the fragment of the Serpent further splintered."

"His entire household?" Tezca tried to keep the horror from his voice. "Even the princess?"

"It is as it must be," Itzamma repeated.

They lapsed into silence. Tezca recalled Cayucali's warning, and suddenly wondered whether kingship was worth the price. Perhaps it had all come too easily. Perhaps to be a dog at home was better than to be a prisoner in Kalak Mool.

Hummingbird

Cayucali splayed his hands against the stone. It was hot on his skin, almost too hot to touch.

The Paddock kept men in by permitting them few ways to get out. But tonight, the paddock was more watchful still; rushlights burned at every intersection, every gate was watched, and even old Zolin had cautioned him that any attempt to escape would result in torture. Someone—he thought he knew who—was not disarmed by the willing demeanor he adopted for the feast in his honor.

He pinched his shoulders together and braced his back against the rear wall of the shrine. He had no other ideas. He pushed, driving his back into the wall and his hands into the great fire-lit statue of the Turquoise Serpent. He felt the slightest motion ripple through the stone. He went slack and the statute tipped back into place for a brief moment. Then he surged, pushing again.

The statute tipped slightly further this time. Soon, it rocked back and forth on its stone plinth. After another minute, it was teetering on the edge of its base. The stones of the plinth splintered beneath the pounding, which echoed through the shrine. Still, no one appeared in the doorway.

Then the statute went over. The barbed tail of the Serpent whipped past Cayucali's face. The snarling, upturned snout crashed into the stone floor with a deafening crack and a bellow of choking dust. The stone braziers went tumbling over, spilling hot coals across the room and belching pale ash and black smoke into the air.

Sparks coruscated across his vision. Soon the flames spread to the cotton draperies and offerings of oil beneath the statues of the lesser gods of Kalak Mool. Some of these were wrought in wood, and quickly blackened in the heat of the flame, as did the great beams that crossed the stone ceiling.

Cayucali picked his way across the shrine as the flames spread. Voices cried from without, coming from the left. He strode quickly away to the right. He made his way through halls filling with smoke, staying out of the sight of shouting men who ran toward the burning shrine at the heart of the Paddock.

He came to a small gate that led out of the Paddock into the citadel, into the open air. A heavy lock held the gate shut, and a man with a spear was a silhouette on the other side. Cayucali pushed his arms through the holes in the gate and caught the spearman by the collar. He pulled sharply. The man's head struck the gate and he collapsed into a limp pile at its foot.

Cayucali plucked the bone file he had stolen from the carpenter's shop from his waistband and began to saw at the heavy beam that barred the gate. He quickly gave up the effort; the beam was thick, and made of some hard wood that resisted the teeth of the rasp. He thrust his arms through the gate once more and attempted to force the beam out of its rests. But no matter how he pushed, the rests held it fast, and from that angle he could find no lasting purchase on the beam.

He looked over his shoulder. No one came for him, but

his spine began to prickle at the time he had already spent in such a vulnerable place. He attacked the brackets that held the beam, dragging the file across one until it bit and cut. He worked furiously. The edges of the gate cut into the muscles of his arms. The first bracket broke. One side of the beam fell, the other still held by the other bracket.

He sawed at that one too, levering the file between the beam and the bracket and dragging it back and forth. He began to cut. The file cracked. Then it snapped. The cutting edge tumbled to the ground outside the gate. Cayucali cursed under his breath. He threw the rest of the useless file away and wrapped his hands around the beam. But no matter how he pushed or pulled, he could not free the beam from the bracket, nor crack the bracket itself.

He cursed again, louder this time. The smoke rose around him. Shouting filtered through the dense network of passages behind him. He put his back to the gate and cast about for the fractured remnant of the file, steadying himself for violence. Then he slumped to the floor, sparing a glance for the unconscious guard on the other side. There was no hope, with his back to the wall and the Blue Knives on the way.

Then he heard a voice from behind him. Something poked his shoulder through the gate.

"Get up, cretin," Tezca said. "Stand back from there."

"What—"

"I said get back!" Tezca snarled. He scratched at the remaining bracket with the broken file, swinging his arm furiously. His eyes were fixed in a mania of concentration. Then he dropped the file and pressed his thumbs to the bracket. A sharp crack and a concussion hammered through the gate and ripped through the air where Cayucali had stood. The bracket fractured. The beam clattered to the floor.

Cayucali threw his bulk against the gate and shoved mightily. The beam scraped across the stone as the gate inched open. He blew the air from his lungs and slipped through the crack. Then he was on the other side, out from the prison of the Paddock and once again free under the wheeling heavens.

He found himself face to face with Tezca once again. The boy was tall; taller than Cayucali realized. Almost as tall as he was himself, and he had met few taller. They stared at each other for a moment. What was it about Tezca that had so maddened him only a few weeks ago? He now seemed only a young man thirsty for recognition, unsure how to ask for it.

"I never thought I would say it," Cayucali said. "But I am glad for your spellcasting."

Tezca smiled and, after a moment, stuck his hand out. "I am sorry for how I acted earlier," he said. "I would not see my countryman murdered."

Cayucali clasped Tezca's outstretched hand. "And I would not see a fine young man squandered on the greed of this bloodthirsty spirit."

"Can you get us out of the citadel?"

"I can," Cayucali said. "With some help."

The Night Market

Smoke gusted from the Paddock gate as they fled into the citadel. Reaching tendrils of it clung to their legs and the bitter scent of char was overwhelming. Yet from the outside, but for the dark smoke creeping along the ground, the fire in the Paddock was unnoticeable. Cayucali dragged the senseless guard far enough away from the smoke that he would not be overcome. Then he and Tezca moved down through the citadel as quickly as they could without running.

"You need something to wear," Tezca said. He himself was adorned in finery suitable to the king of Kalak Mool. He wore a tunic and cloak of thick cotton, dyed white and embroidered in threads of citrine yellow and cardinal red. In his hair were the long emerald feathers of the quetzal. He stripped them out and threw them into the gutter.

"Give me your cloak," Cayucali said.

Tezca swung the white cloak from his shoulders and threw it to Cayucali. Cayucali draped it over his shoulders, but it was cut for a much smaller man and covered neither his height nor his breadth.

"No good," Cayucali said.

"There is a market not far from here," Tezca said.

They followed the winding alleys and passages further down the mountainside. The streets were empty and silent for much of the way, growing populous only as they approached a bright square that rang with the sound of commerce.

Reed canopies filled the square in a chaotic profusion of stalls where merchants offered the bounty of Kalak Mool for sale; carpets and other things woven on the loom, furniture wrought in wicker and soft wood, food cooked and uncooked in a hundred varieties.

There was a row of merchants selling the beads and earrings that marked social status in Kalak Mool, from leather and common woods to noble gold and priestly turquoise. In another cluster of stalls, men and women did a ferocious trade in the bones of certain animals, which some supposed to retain the alchemical properties of the animal's life.

When they found the avenue where clothes were sold, Tezca traded one of his own golden ear plugs to a tailor and gestured at Cayucali, who ended up with a serviceable outfit much less valuable than the golden plug. But he would not stand out.

They left the night market by the far end of the square and came to a crossroads, where they halted through some unspoken agreement. Tezca glanced first upward, then down the hill toward the valley and the river.

"There is something you must hear," Tezca said.

"There is nothing I want to hear except how to get out of this accursed citadel."

"I know how to get out of the citadel," Tezca said. "And you can defend us, if there are not too many soldiers. But I do not know the way to Batun. And neither do you. And Oahqui and the Blue Knives know these lands well. They will find you missing, then they will find me missing, then they will look for us. Then we will not be missing—we will be dead."

Cayucali frowned and crossed his arms. "So what do we do?"

"The other thing is that you were right. Itzamma was keeping something from me, and so was Yax Yapaat. For me to become king, they must sacrifice Yax Yapaat—and his entire household with him."

"Then, Xhoc?"

Tezca nodded.

Cayucali suddenly laughed. "I see your plan, you devil. You have found yourself a higher prize than kingship!"

Tezca blushed, but did not look away. "She is kind to me. She thinks I am a good man."

"And she is beautiful," Cayucali said. "Even an old boar like me can see that."

"She is beautiful," Tezca admitted. "I would not have her butchered for any reason, and could not—I would not want to gain from such a sacrifice. Not hers, and not yours."

Cayucali studied Tezca for a moment, then put his hand on the wizard's shoulder. "We will go back for her," he said. "If you think she will come away with us."

"She will," Tezca said. "I am certain. If not for herself, if not for me, than for you. She has great love for you."

"Yax Yapaat and I were not dissimilar, once," Cayucali said. "She loved her father, and now he is lost to her. You are right to love her. She is a fine woman. And you are right to bring her with us. She knows the lands of the Kalak Mool. So then, where is she?"

"In the palace complex. She had rooms near mine. I can bring us there, but there are many guards. Itzamma has the entire palace working to prepare for the coronation."

"I have an idea," Cayucali said. "Take us to the palace. I will explain."

Tezca led them around the corner, up the hill toward the

royal palace. They had taken only a few steps when a sharp command cracked the quiet.

"You two," the voice said. "Stop."

Cayucali shared a meaningful glance with Tezca. They stopped, and turned to face their pursuer. He stalked toward them through the shadow of the building, a blurred silhouette that only slowly resolved itself into the shape of a large man. He had only one arm.

"Zolin?" Cayucali asked softly.

"Cayucali," Zolin said. "You survived the fire. A blessing in the face of great tragedy. The statue of Xicuoatl is broken beyond repair."

"I will not return to the Paddock, Zolin," Cayucali said.

"The serpent guard searches for you. They found no body. They know you did not perish in the blaze."

"Yet it is you who found me. Again."

There was a long pause before Zolin stepped forward again. The white moonlight fell on his face. He bore a small pack over his shoulder.

"Some of them search this street, nearer the Paddock. You will cross their path if you are not careful. Allow me to guide you. It would be an honor to serve in your command." Zolin made a gesture of subservience.

"You honor me," Cayucali said. "I command nothing. But I welcome the aid of a friend."

"I dreamt of my old farm," Zolin said. "I cannot buy enough tobacco to repay you for my life. I will have to grow it. You will come and visit me, and we will smoke while the sun sets."

"Come," Tezca said. "There will be time later for friendship."

The three threaded a careful path up the hill under the diamond moonlight, through the serpent-haunted citadel, toward the palace of the King of Kalak Mool.

The Center

Kalak Mool was a land of rings within rings. At its center was the great citadel, the mountain upon the mountain. The citadel itself revolved upon the axis of the royal palace, where dwelt the King, his household, favored nobility, and the highest of the priestly class.

And at the heart of the sprawling royal palace, yet another mountain stood. The Temple of the Serpent was the most sacred of the many shrines made to the many gods of Kalak Mool, and used only for the highest rituals.

It was that black heart toward which Cayucali and Tezca now moved. The ways into the palace were not guarded. In Kalak Mool, no one visited the palace without reason.

They came into the palace quickly and moved freely though the many avenues and buildings. Tezca lead them past his own quarters, where he stopped for a brief moment to retrieve some small items, and then toward the suite of rooms that belonged to Xhoc.

Two Blue Knives guarded Xhoc's doors. Cayucali and Tezca watched them from around a far corner. Cayucali dragged a finger across his throat, but Tezca shook his head. He showed Cayucali the thing he retrieved from his own quarters: a small leather pouch full of a greenish powder. Cayucali raised his eyebrows.

"Burundanga," Tezca whispered.

Then, the pouch hidden in his palm, he stood and turned the corner before Cayucali could stop him. He sauntered down the hall toward Xhoc's rooms, letting his heels scuff on the stone floor, alerting the Blue Knives. The two drew their blades immediately and ordered him to stop.

Tezca smiled and shook his head. "No, I am only here to visit the princess, she and I must discuss tonight's ritual—"

"The King has ordered no one—" the first man said, and nothing else.

When Tezca drew close enough, he flung his arm in a wide arc and emptied the pouch of burundanga into the faces of the Blue Knives. The two collapsed almost instantly, twitching briefly then going still, their eyes unfocused and their jaws slack.

Cayucali and Zolin took up positions of watchfulness along the hall while Tezca knocked quietly on Xhoc's door. His heart raced. There was no answer. He knocked again, louder. There was the soft sound of footfalls on the other side. Then a timid voice calling through the door.

"Who is there?"

"It is Tezca. Please, open quickly."

Xhoc cracked the heavy wooden door. Tezca put his hand against it to push it open, but she held it fast from the far side.

"What is it?" she asked. "Why do you come? Have you forgotten what must happen later in the night?"

"I have not forgotten," Tezca said. "It is that which I must talk to you about. Please, open!"

Xhoc frowned. "Itzamma would not—"

A huge hand appeared on the door beside Tezca's head. The door slammed open when Cayucali pushed. Xhoc stumbled back, gasping in fear. She staggered back, clutching at an armoir to keep from falling. She opened her mouth wide to scream as the giant Cayucali shouldered through the doorway, followed by the one-armed Zolin.

Tezca rushed to her, pressing his hand over her mouth and looking her in the eyes as Zolin and Cayucali dragged the two senseless Blue Knives into the room and closed the door behind them. Her eyes were wide above his hand, but she did not scream. She met his stare and nodded. He pulled his hand away and clasped her narrow shoulders.

"I am leaving," Tezca said. "We all are."

"But," Xhoc whispered "The coalescence, your coronation—it is near. Your time is close."

"I would not gain the Waterlily Throne, nor anything else in this world, if it comes at the cost of your life."

"My life?" Xhoc wondered. "It is my father who must—" She fell silent as understanding dawned. Her eyes filled with tears. She looked away.

"I see," she said. "As the father goes, so goes his household. I had hoped . . . but this is the way of Kalak Mool. What good will it do to flee? Itzamma will find another vessel. Yax Yapaat spoke for me long ago. We move on our orbits, like the planets."

"Come with us," Tezca said. "You know these lands. When two planets collide, their orbits must change. I need your help. Please."

Xhoc was silent for a moment, then nodded to herself and flew into motion. She withdrew a large leather satchel from the armoir behind her and began to stuff it, all the while speaking in a loud whisper.

"I will come," she said. "My life has been a preparation for death and I do not fear it, or to make a sacrifice of myself. But I would not offer myself for the cruelties and amusements of the Turquoise Serpent. Itzamma slew my father many years ago when he made him king. I will leave, so that I may one day return. I do this favor for you that one day, you may aid me in my need."

She plucked the golden ear plugs from her ears and the emerald feathers from her hair and tucked them into the satchel. She dumped the glittering contents of a stone jewelry box in after them. She removed her fine slippers and put on the same dusty walking sandals she had worn in the aviary. She wrapped herself in an undyed cloak of plain weave, a commoner's travel garment.

"Let us not tarry," she said.

Tezca nearly wept in relief. Instead, he simply knelt and touched his forehead to the floor. Then he sprang to his feet and embraced her giddily.

"I too am glad for your company," Cayucali said. "And gladder still I do not have to carry you out of here."

Xhoc scowled at him. "You think you know what is best for me?"

"I know that I know," Cayucali said gravely.

He stripped the long, lapis cloak from one of the Blue Knives while Zolin undressed the other.

"And what is best is for us to leave now. We must put some strides between us and the citadel before our pursuit comes."

The jovial mood sobered, and all nodded. They crept from Xhoc's rooms in single file, Cayucali at the head of the column and Zolin at the tail, each dressed in the garb of the palace guard. Xhoc and Tezca whispered back and forth concerning which route was safest, and whether they should turn here left and there right. The shortest way out of the citadel led them through the center of the palace complex. Cayucali did not like the risk, but the stars were fading; dawn was near.

The disguises would fool no one for long, but several times they slipped past inattentive guards who offered them only cursory inspections. The color of the cloak was enough to allay suspicion and avoid interest. They had come nearly to the Temple of the Serpent, an imposing ziggurat that dominated the palace complex with its menacing presence.

A handful of shapes emerged from the darkness ahead of them; a band of men in lapis cloaks, walking toward them. Cayucali pulled his hood lower over his face and led his little troop to the side of the path to let the larger column pass. As they drew abreast, the leader of the troop studyied them carefully. Cayucali groaned as the hooded face turned toward him; it was Oahqui.

Shock rippled across the Commander's face, then fury. He snapped out a command, and his column suddenly bristled with long ceremonial spears, their polished blackglass points forming a deadly necklace around Cayucali, Tezca, Xhoc, and Zolin.

"How thoughtful," Oahqui said, mastering himself. "You spare me the trouble of collecting you one by one."

Celestial Agreement

※

"The hour is here," Oahqui said. "The ritual awaits you there, at the crown of the Temple. Now walk, or we will drag you."

The walk to the Temple of the Turquoise Serpent was not long, but time seemed to expand into eternity by the time Tezca's foot hit the first stone stair. The stairs were ancient, polished and worn down by the tread of feet climbing up and stained dark with the flow of blood spilling down.

To each side of the long, steep stair, fires burned in shallow stone reservoirs. The flames lit their climb in lurid shades of coral, nasturtium and topaz. Their climb was slow and silent but for the moaning wind and susurrating flames, but their shadows danced around them, whirling and gyring to some mad music.

Oahqui led the column. The long hilt of Cayucali's sword protruded over his shoulder like a taunt. His Blue Knives followed them. The blackglass points of their spears drank in the firelight and churned with malice. Their destination was familiar to Cayucali. There, weeks past, they had their first audience with Yax Yapaat before the Waterlily Throne.

There, nights past, the nobility of Kalak Mool held a feast in his honor.

At the top of the stair, the ziggurat flattened into a broad stone plane. At the center of the plane was a rounded stone altar like the one Tezca had seen in the ruins. At its base was a deep basin.

Yax Yapaat stood behind the table, Itzamma to one side. Both were gowned in white tunics and draped in formal cloaks dyed in colors commensurate with their status. Yax Yapaat wore gold rings on each of his fingers. White-clad priests hovered over still forms in the shadows. Tezca recognized one of them, and suddenly realized they were the other members of Yax Yapaat's household. Now, their blood filled the basin of the altar.

Itzamma faced them. His face showed first confusion, then grief.

"You have reconsidered your decision," he said sadly. "No matter. The time has come. There is no way back to the way things were, no matter what any of us may wish for. There are powers in this world greater than us; powers which use us as resources the same way we use the animals, the plants, the stones and the earth. They set us upon our orbits, and we obey."

"I will say little else," he continued. "The ritual of coalescence begins with me. The first cut is mine."

Itzamma lifted a blackglass blade. It shimmered in the light of the flames that burned at each corner of the square. An evil, suppurating presence inhabited the incense that rolled from the fires. He drew the blade across the palm of his hand. Blood pooled and dripped down his arms.

"I believe you will find this instructive, Tezca. You have an instinct for this sorcery. It is satisfying in a way dry sigilry never could be, is it not?"

"The price is too high," Tezca said.

"Yet the contract cannot be unmade," Itzamma said,

"except at a cost far higher still. A cost I will not pay."

"I will not be king," Tezca said.

Itzamma closed his hand and drew upon his own blood until it dispersed in a plume of black ash. Oahqui gestured. The Blue Knives prodded Tezca forward until he stood across the altar from Yax Yapaat. Itzamma pressed his hand to the altar then sagged, buckling at the knees. Something passed from him into the altar.

Yax Yapaat bent forward. His eyes were unfocused, his expression blank. Itzamma rose to his feet shakily, favoring his injured leg. He extended the blackglass blade to Tezca.

"Take it," he said. "Cut his throat. Spill his life's blood on the altar."

Tezca took the knife. The corded hilt was coarse in his palm. Yax Yapaat's face was expressionless. He stood above the altar, docile as a lamb. Tezca looked over his shoulder to where Cayucali stood beside Xhoc. Xhoc wept openly, her face buried in her hands.

Cayucali swung his head slowly. "No," he rumbled.

Oahqui slammed the flat of the ironwood blade into Cayucali's legs. The huge warrior fell to his knees.

"Quiet," Oahqui said. "Your time is coming."

"Your time will come first," Cayucali said.

"Make the cut," Itzamma whispered.

"No," Tezca said. He shook his head. He let the knife fall from his hand. The blackglass blade shattered against the stone. "I will not."

Itzamma smirked. His hand vanished into his cloak and emerged bearing another blade.

"Very well," he said. "It matters not who makes the cut."

He grasped the back of Yax Yapaat's head with one hand and drew the blade across the king's throat. Black blood flooded from Yax Yapaat's throat and drenched the stone altar. It gathered in the basin beneath the altar, dark and still as the deep sea. Xhoc sobbed into her hands.

The king's body was stiff, his eyes empty. His skin was ghastly and white. He twitched and jerked, bending backward and turning his face to the sky. The wind rose around them, eerie wails that gusted droplets of stinging rain across the square. The altar quivered with power, drawing the world into itself as the gaunt form of Yax Yapaat stood rigid above it.

Yax Yapaat flung his arms wide and arched his back unnaturally. His head was heavy behind him; the weight of it opened the wound in his neck wider. Pearlescent smoke poured from that wound, erupting from his belly like a gray whale's spout and filling the air above him. The smoke did not disperse, but instead coalesced.

Yax Yapaat's body emptied. The final tendril of smoke drifted into the roiling mass above them. As it spun and writhed, a rainbow of deadly colors scintillated in its depths; the colors of gangrene and rot, the colors of bloodstains and buzzardkill. Tezca sensed a pattern to its motion, a sinuous winding, an infinite twisting and coiling.

Itzamma's acolytes lifted the corpse of Yax Yapaat and laid it out on the stone, making long cuts down down his belly and across the inside of his arms and legs, peeling his skin away with gentle tugs and careful slices. Another sawed through the bones of his wrists until his hands came away.

"The Turquoise Serpent," Itzamma said, staring at Tezca. "Or that fragment of him inherited by the Kings of Kalak Mool. The first movement of the ritual is complete. Commander Oahqui—the Champion."

Oahqui barked. Two of the Blue Knives seized Tezca. Four more took hold of Cayucali and dragged him forward. They pushed him over the rounded altar, bending his back against the curve. One took hold of each limb and knelt to the floor.

"The second movement can now begin,'" Itzamma said.

He lifted the blackglass blade and stepped toward the altar.

The Coronation Rite of the Turquoise Serpent

The pinnacle of the Temple of the Serpent had held many feasts, and now it held another. Now, the Turquoise Serpent would feed on Cayucali.

The edge of the blade parted flesh at a touch. Cayucali clenched his jaw as Itzamma made a careful cut along one wrist. Though he struggled mightily, the Blue Knives held him fast to the altar.

"Every drop of the Champion's blood must be preserved," Itzamma said.

His priestly attendants, having completed their grisly harvest of Yax Yapaat's remains, now knelt beside the altar. As the blood drained from Cayucali's wrist, they guided each drop in its course to fall in the basin beneath the altar.

"His strength must be preserved."

Oahqui drove Tezca to his knees before the altar. Xhoc and Zolin were made to kneel also. Above them, the fragment of the Serpent whirled and smoked and seemed to grow more concrete, more fully real. The tendrils of smoke coalesced into fleeting impressions of thick coils and bright scales before dispersing back into colored smoke again.

"Yax Yapaat's blood makes one half of the bridge," Itzamma said.

His voice rose above the wind, his hawk's eyes were feverish in the firelight.

"The Champion's blood," he continued, "the other half. And what a fine Champion we have cultivated for you, Tezca. An auspicious omen for the beginning of your reign. What will your regnal name be, I wonder?"

"If you make me king, I shall have you executed immediately," Tezca shouted. "I shall tear down the Temple of the Serpent and by edict purge his worship from Kalak Mool. I shall make alliance with Batun by eradicating the practice of blood sorcery!"

Itzamma only laughed.

"No," he said. "You shall not. Yax Yapaat said such things to me when he knelt where you now kneel. Like you, he had not the humility to recognize that to share your body, your soul, with a great one such as the Serpent is to *serve*. To be subjugated. But like you will, he became more than himself. No, you shall not execute me. The Serpent has use for me yet."

Tezca hung his head. He stared at the stones of the Temple, full of despair. Xhoc begged him to do something, anything. But there was nothing to be done. Itzamma extended the cut a little further up Cayucali's arm. More blood flowed into the basin, where it boiled and smoked and burned away into black ash. The fragment of the Serpent above them began to tremble and turn toward Tezca.

A pale line in the stone caught Tezca's eye. It meant something to him. He turned his head to follow it and discovered a sigil etched into the stone. His sigil, scratched idly into the stone during their first audience with Yax Yapaat upon coming to Kalak Mool what seemed like a lifetime ago. The colored smoke of the snake god wreathed him now; he nearly choked on the thick, lily-flower fragrance. Strange visions filled his head.

His sigil. He sought Cayucali's eye. The huge warrior had ceased to struggle against his captors and now watched the scene with disgust. Tezca's fixed stare caught his gaze soon enough, and the warrior's face softened into a question. Tezca closed his eyes deliberately, then turned his head away. Then he caught Cayucali's gaze again and repeated the gesture. Then a third time. Cayucali nodded his understanding. He closed his own eyes, and turned his face away.

Tezca lunged forward, wresting his arms from the grasp of the Blue Knives who held him. He scrambled toward the altar. The Blue Knives fell upon him in an instant, pinning him to the ground. He ripped one arm free. He plunged it into the bloody basin. It came out glistening and black, coated in Cayucali's blood. As the Blue Knives wrestled him away from the altar, he dragged his bloodstained hand across the sigil he had drawn weeks ago and whispered the word of activation.

Then he closed his eyes, and turned his head away. Despite this precaution, the explosion of gemstone flames nearly blinded him. Every color he had ever seen, saturated to painful intensity, screamed across his vision and illuminated the dark night. There was a blast, a pulse of force that sent men tumbling through the air and skidding along the stone of the temple. The sound of wind buffeted his ears as air rushed to fill the hole the flames burned in the sky.

The smoky fragment of the Turquoise Serpent dispersed, scattered by the wind into mere wisps of fog, and then into nothing. The sense of immanent presence, the nearness of the terrible *mind* of Xiuhcoatl was gone. There was a residual feeling of frustration, of anger, and perhaps an echo of laughter...

When Tezca opened his eyes, Cayucali had thrown off the Blue Knives who still clung to him. Several lay in broken shapes, or facedown in now pooling blood. Cayucali stalked to where Oahqui lay senseless on the stone and picked up his great ironwood blade. He stared at the fallen Blue Knife with black intent, then leapt to where Xhoc and Zolin had fallen.

"Tezca, help me get them up. We must get out of the citadel. What is the shortest route?"

"The Gate of the Lake," Tezca said. "Down the Avenue of the King. We can cross the river and enter the forest. There is a pass on the far side of the vale."

"No," Xhoc said. "Tezca, no. They will catch us. They will guess we went that way."

"Then which way?" Cayucali hissed.

"The aviary," she said.

"Aviary?"

"She is right," Tezca said. "There is a hidden valley, a secret way through the mountains, out of Kalak Mool."

"Can you lead us, Princess?" Cayucali asked.

"I cannot see," she said. "Only shadows."

"I know the way," Tezca said. "Some of it."

"Lead on," Zolin said. "As far as you can. Our vision will return. You can describe what Princess Xhoc cannot see. But let us go. Those still alive here will recover soon, and others will come."

Cayucali shouldered his heavy sword. "I agree. We must go swiftly."

"But," Xhoc said. "The aviary leads only to the great wilderness to the south. I do not know those lands. No one has come through them alive."

"Then we shall be the first," Cayucali said.

The Warlord

❦

They put the Temple of the Serpent to their backs and fled through the palace, deep into the mountain. Cayucali took the rearguard position, checking over his shoulder constantly for pursuit. None came.

Wrong turns devoured precious moments more than once. As Xhoc's vision returned, she put them on the right course. Now she led Tezca, Zolin, and Cayucali into the mountain with great confidence. They wound through disused halls and dusty warehouses where huge spiders spun thick webs. Cayucali shrugged. It was not the way he would have gone, but then, where better to put a hidden passage out of the city?

"Through here," Xhoc said. "The hall turns. Around the corner, we will rejoin the passage to the Aviary. You remember now, Tezca."

Tezca nodded. He took the lead, and led Xhoc around the corner. Zolin too disappeared around the corner, then shouted in alarm. Cayucali pounded through the empty storeroom and around the corner at last. He found himself in a broad hallway, well-lit and softened with a fine carpet beneath his feet. At the end of the hall was an arched doorway open to the cool air of mountain night.

Oahqui placed himself between them and the doorway. He held Xhoc by the wrist. Tezca lay against the wall, groaning and clutching his skull. His hands were red.

"Zolin," Cayucali snapped at the one-armed soldier. "Stand away. Let us hear what he wants."

Oahqui pressed the point of his spear into Xhoc's spine. "And what should I want, slave, but the return of escaped slaves and sacrifices?"

"For what? The stars have changed. The time of the agreement is past. The thing in the smoke is gone, back to wherever such things lurk and breed. You know this better than I do."

Oahqui nodded. "You are clever," he said. "Cleverer than you look. But I suppose you must be clever, to have lived so long, Warlord. Yes, I know you now! The famed Warlord Cayucali, now Champion of Kalak Mool. A suitable nemesis. I will mount your blade above my hearth. I will wear your hands with great pride."

"You will have to take them yourself," Cayucali said. He lifted his sword from his shoulder and let the tip rest against the floor of the passage. "I do not think you can. If you could, I would have heard of you."

Oahqui snarled at the goad. He threw Xhoc aside and rushed toward Cayucali. Zolin reached out to stop Oahqui, but the Blue Knife shouldered the old soldier aside with ease. His head hammered against the wall, and he collapsed.

The duel began with a spear thrust like a bolt of lightning. Sheer instinct saved Cayucali from that lance; he fell backward away from the point, stumbling until he caught his footing once again. Oahqui came forward again. Cayucali lifted his blade.

When he did, he grimaced. The stinging cut on his arm and the tremble in his legs reminded him of the blood

Itzamma took from him. The spear flashed again and again, its black point plunging and striking like the head of a viper. Cayucali swung the heavy ironwood blade, turning away blow after blow, but the razor edge of the spearhead caught him more than once. Blood he could ill afford to lose seeped from his wounds.

Oahqui pressed his advantage. His expression was wild. He sought to overwhelm Cayucali with a vicious and dizzying tangle of attacks. His spear was like a forest. Yet Cayucali defended against the onslaught. The ironwood blade twitched and Cayucali slipped and twisted around it, avoiding the hungry black fang. But there was no break in the rain of blows, and any opportunity to counterattack was beyond the ability of his weary shoulders. It was all he could do to stay alive.

The spear paused for a moment. Cayucali sensed the opening and brought his blade forward to attack. He recognized his own trap a moment too late. Oahqui's grim smile widened. His hand flickered, and his blue stone knife spun twice before burying itself in Cayucali's shoulder, just above his heart. The force of the blow nearly spun him on his feet. He caught himself with the point of his blade. Oahqui took up his spear again and stalked forward.

Cayucali reached for the knife, then thought better of it.

"You may as well," Oahqui said. "I would not want to damage my own blade. I am going to put my spear just a little bit low—"

"You will not," someone said. Zolin was up again. He put himself between Oahqui and Cayucali.

"I will," Oahqui said. "However many other slaves I must put down first."

"I am not a slave," Zolin said. He spoke slowly, emphasizing each word, as drew himself to his full height. "If I have lived as a slave, I will die as a free man of Kapan."

"If you say so," Oahqui said. He thrust the spear casually,

almost contemptuously, into Zolin's chest. The old man gave a little gasp as the blackglass blade cut through skin and scraped across bone. Blood welled at the edges of the blade. His face went pale.

Zolin caught the neck of the spear in his one good hand. He sagged to his knees, dragging the spear down with him. Oahqui followed forward, pushing the head of the spear deeper into Zolin's chest and twisting it. Zolin coughed bubbles of pink blood. His knuckles were white around the haft of the spear.

"Trivial old cripple," Oahqui spat, already staring at Cayucali. He pulled his spear back, but it did not budge. He frowned, glancing down at the dying Zolin. The old man smiled. His thick hand held the neck of the spear like a vice. Oahqui's eyes widened. He turned his head back toward Cayucali.

The ironwood blade shattered through the bones of Oahqui's neck in one murderous swing. His severed head spun away, painting the walls with viscera. Lines of hot blood splattered Cayucali's face and he smiled. Oahqui's headless corpse fell backward. The spear clattered backward with it as Zolin's hand finally opened.

Cayucali knelt. "You might have lived, old man," he said.

"Doubt it," Zolin said. "Better to do something useful with it."

"They will honor you in Kapan."

"That would be nice," he said, coughing out more blood. "Nicer if you found someone to take care of my little farm. Warlord—in my pocket—"

Cayucali pulled a folded tobacco leaf from Zolin's pocket. It was drenched in blood. Then Zolin spasmed once. His last breath rattled from his chest as blood drained from the wound in his chest.

Cayucali tucked the bloody tobacco leaf away, then roused

Xhoc and Tezca. Together, they passed through the gate and into the open sky of the aviary.

Before Dawn

❧

"Can you make light?" Xhoc asked.

Tezca shook his head. "We cannot risk it."

"It is hard to see the path," she said. The high canopy of the hidden valley blocked the starlight and hid them from the sight of the full moon. Chirping crickets fell silent as they passed, then began their song again.

Once, Tezca strayed near the nest of a tinamou and leapt in fright as the olive-colored bird spread its wings wide and shrieked at him. Cayucali and Xhoc were too nervous to laugh.

"As long as we walk south," Tezca said. "We will come to the cliff. We will have the moonlight then."

Cayucali nodded. He walked behind Tezca and Xhoc. He probed gently at the knife still lodged in his shoulder. The blood flow had stopped. He thought the blade missed his arteries. He hoped Tezca and Xhoc knew where to go; he could hardly keep up with them, much less lead them through unfamiliar territory.

Things could have been worse, he reckoned. He had considered simply kidnapping Tezca and dragging him back to Batun. That would have been a miserable journey. This was better. So far, the boy had behaved himself. The princess had a powerful effect on him.

They came out from under the trees at the place where the hidden path descended the escarpment. Xhoc found the trailhead in the light of the moon. Cayucali's sharp eyes picked out the exposed turns of the disguised trail. His gaze lifted to the dense jungle at the base of the escarpment, and to the dark wilderness beyond.

"Let us not tarry," Cayucali said, gesturing for them to proceed.

"You must let me attend your wound," Xhoc said.

"We have no time, no medicine," Cayucali said. "And I have gone farther with worse."

He ripped a long strip of fabric from his cloak. Then he reached across his chest and removed the blade with one steady pull. It came forth with a sucking sound. He clenched his jaw against the pain. Blood came, but only sluggishly. He pressed his makeshift bandage against the wound. Xhoc tied it over his shoulder and beneath his arm.

He flipped the blade around in his hand and offered the hilt to Tezca.

"Take it," he said. "You may need it. At worst, you will have something to recall to you that you were once King of Kalak Mool."

"I suppose I still am," Tezca said.

They were not long beneath the canopy of the dense jungle when they began to hear certain familiar sounds. Shadowy forms crept through the trees above them, chattering boldly to each other. Eyes gleamed from darkness deeper than the leaves. What followed them had grown bolder.

"We should have followed the eaves of the forest," Tezca said.

"The men of Kalak Mool are faster than us on foot," Cayucali said. "We must hide our trail."

"It was a sound strategy," Tezca said. "But the jungle has dangers at night. I fear we face worse than Blue Knives now."

Even as he said it, a dark shape crashed through the canopy. Small branches cracked. There was a sound of leather like a bellows as black wings snapped wide. A hideous face, with manic eyes set above a bestial, upturned snout and gleaming bone-white fangs fell upon Cayucali.

It drove him to the soft floor of the jungle. It snapped its ravening jaws open and shut above him, gnawing the air above his throat and slavering on his throat. He held it by the shoulders. Its wide wings enfolded him; sharp claws clutched at him.

Then the beast shuddered and died. Cayucali rolled its fetid carcass off him and climbed to his feet. Tezca put his foot to the beast's spine and tugged until the blue stone blade came free of its skull. Cayucali studied the creature at his feet. It resembled nothing so much as a gargantuan bat. He craned his head to study the branches above them.

"Ugly," Tezca said. He wiped the blade on the beast's furred breast.

"We should go," Xhoc said.

There was movement in the shadows above.

"I agree," Cayucali said, his voice tense. "Run!"

They ran. The forest above them was suddenly alive with deadly motion. Hungry eyes burned in the darkness. Broad wings and grasping claws spiraled through the leaves to fall upon them.

Tezca lashed about himself with his knife. The monstrous bat-things screeched and fell back for a moment, nursing the clean wounds opened by the sharp blade.

Cayucali swung the ironwood sword one-handed, but his weary arm lacked the strength to do more than bruise the savage beasts, and the long blade caught on clinging vines and branches. More of the creatures came.

The jungle floor was now thick with them. They clung to

the holes of trees and crept along the ground on four limbs with a stiff and ungainly gait. Soon, the three were surrounded. The bat-things crowed in excitement, sending up strange piercing cries that raise goosebumps along their skin.

Then a huge shape exploded through the jungle canopy. The sound of branches breaking was like lightning striking. The great war-song of the condor was like a thousand ram's horn trumpets blown by the thousand heralds of some heaven-dwelling king. The enormous raptor clawed and winged its way to the floor of the jungle like a cormorant diving for fish.

It snapped up three of the bat-things in its pale beak, severing flesh and bone with equal ease. It scattered more of them with claws like reaping blades. The great beating of its wings was a wind that drove the bat-things away into the trees. The clarion call rang out again, and the bat-things fled in fear, abandoning the torn bodies of their fellows to the colossal bird.

Tezca stared at the condor in awe. As the creatures fled into the forest, Cayucali lifted Xhoc to her feet.

"Tezca," he hissed. "Come!"

The condor lowered its head to Tezca, offering him a knowing and amused stare.

"It knows me," he said. "What does that mean?"

"Think about it later!" Xhoc said, pulling at his arm. With a final glance toward the condor, Tezca turned and followed Xhoc and Cayucali through the trees.

Toward the Sun

They stumbled into the morning almost without realizing it. The southern line of the forest met a vast golden plain in a sharp line that stretched across the prairie. High grasses swayed in the gentle winds like ripples in a pond. On the far horizon, a blurry gray smudge marked a distant mountain range. The sun rose in the east, climbing out of the sea that lay somewhere to their left.

"We have left the lands of Kalak Mool," Xhoc said. "I do not think anyone will pursue us this far. Though I do not doubt Itzamma will dream some terrible fate for us if we should fall into his grasp. He is a patient hunter."

"Good," Tezca said. "Then we are free to return to Batun."

Cayucali scoffed.

"No one will pursue us because there is nothing in this wilderness," Xhoc said. "They believe we will die here, as everyone who comes here does. We cannot cross the mountains unless we walk all the way around—months and months, and I do not know the way. We cannot go to Batun, except through Kalak Mool."

"Then we are lost," Tezca said. "Will we die here?"

Cayucali fished something from his cloak. The tobacco leaf. He unfolded the leaf. A handful of cigars tumbled out into his palm. Cayucali smiled.

"We will not," he said. He passed the tobacco leaf to Xhoc. "Look at this."

Xhoc looked at Cayucali in amazement. "The old man?" She handed the leaf to Tezca.

"He saved us twice," Cayucali said.

"A map," Tezca said. "But where does it lead? What is this symbol?"

"It is the sun," Xhoc said, in awe. "The golden kingdom of the Gods of the Sun. We go to Chimor!"

Tezca glanced at Cayucali.

Cayucali shrugged. "Chimal can wait a while longer to claim my head. I have always wanted to see the truth of Chimor for myself."

"And I am in no haste to face Master Tall Deer's scolding," Tezca said with a rakish smile.

They set off, wading into the shimmering sea of grass bearing south, toward the distant mountains. From the jungle behind them, a dark shape climbed into the sky on silent wings. It circled above them three times, then soared southward riding the warm wind, dwindling, then vanishing into the horizon.

About the Author

"If you are what you should be, you will set the whole world ablaze!"

-St. Catherine of Siena

Also by Alexander Palacio

The Lord of the Bottom of the Earth

Made in the USA
Las Vegas, NV
08 January 2024

84074389R00100